Copyright ©

Redwood Massacre and ass
© 2020 Clear Focus Movies and used under licence

All rights reserved

The characters and events portrayed in this book are fictitious. Any similarity to real persons, living or dead, is coincidental and not intended by the author.

No part of this book may be reproduced, or stored in a retrieval system, or transmitted in any form or by any means, electronic, mechanical, photocopying, recording, or otherwise, without express written permission of the publisher.

For Dad

# INTRODUCTION

It is like a black hole which exists purely for your emotions and emotional wellbeing, a gravitational pull which absorbs all light in your life into a darkness than has unfathomable depths. There is no respite from the torment, no relief from the pain. You descend ever further, scrambling to pull yourself out but without the physical or mental strength to do so. The agonising tearing at your soul is endless and tortuous.

In polite society we do not know how to talk about such depravity of feeling, so we bundle it all up into one easy to understand word; grief.

It has been ten years since I last saw my daughter alive. Ten years where I have had to consider the events, or the reported events, of one haunting weekend. A weekend from which families have had to accept that they will never see their loved ones again. A weekend whose events we all must live with while not actually knowing the truth. A weekend of mayhem, bloodlust, murder, and mystery.

My daughter was the most beautiful and intelligent woman I had ever met. As a father it is my job to say that, and to believe it. My other job as a father is to protect my daughter and there I failed. Fathers should not outlive their daughters. Despite all I could give her, I could not give her safety, or a life of any acceptable length. What she got instead was a short, happy life that was ended in the most violent manner.

The truth is a hard word to use under these circumstances. Facts are missing, and the police have given no truths. This, to them at least, is a missing person's case. A bright, beautiful young woman has gone missing in the unforgiving mountains. One of many beautiful daughters, and strong sons. Of brave fathers and loving mothers. For almost all these events were started by a camping trip, in an area of unparalleled beauty and unequivocal danger. What should be a trip which delights and brings people closer together inevitably descends into horror. The depths of those horrors we are yet to fully grasp.

What we have are many missing persons, little known facts, a plethora of stories and legends and gaping wounds ripping apart so many families.

My investigation has done nothing to remedy these wounds, not to heal them nor to provide some salve to lessen the sting. What it has achieved is to shine a bright and punishing light into the ineptitude of the local police force, to highlight a town drenched in fear of a legend and to further drive me in my quest for truth and ultimately, for justice.

As a father I am broken, as a man I feel weak. I will never be able to start piecing my life back together until I have found answers. The damage done to me and to other families is exacerbated by the absence of fact, the absence of bodies and the absence of closure.

This book documents my journey so far. Its sole purpose is to bring to the public consciousness the horrific truth around the Redwood Forest so that one day the truth will out. I have lost everything on my journey so far. Family, friends, my job, and my home. It is the price I am willing to pay to ensure that my daughter gets her final chapter, and that it is written by someone who loves her.

# CHAPTER 1

When you are in the moment all mornings seem much the same. You follow your routine, usually consisting of a shower and a brush of your teeth, and the unmentionable toilet requirements. You apply your chosen deodorant to mask your natural scent, put on your clothes and show your face to the world. The morning of June 6th, 2010 was not different. It was a Saturday, so the only tangible difference for me was the outfit I placed myself into. Instead of the suit, the tie, and loafers I was in jeans, a "dad" t-shirt as my daughter would so delightfully tease, and a pair of sneakers. Other than that, this was a very normal day.

As was usual I would make myself breakfast and shout upstairs to see if anyone else wanted some. Occasionally I would get some sort of grunted reply, but rarely a confirmation of anything specific. Never would I get a response that one could truly refer to as human communication. As such it was breakfast for one. I always accepted the inevitability that I would by making more breakfast in the coming hours, as requested, or sometimes expected. Eggs were my go-to food. Easy to make, you just crack them, scramble them, and swallow them. Efficient, healthy, and full of flavour. Or at least full of flavour when you add some salt, pepper, and a little fresh chilli powder.

The fridge was well stocked as always just in case my world view of eggs as staple breakfast sustenance was not shared by the other house occupants.

Sarah was always like clockwork when she got up. By that I do not mean that she kept good time hygiene with when she rose, but I could guarantee as soon as I sat down to my second cup of coffee she would appear at the top of the stairs. Now I was not regimented with my second cup of java. There could be anything from thirty minutes to an hour between cup one and cup two. Sarah always had the uncanny knack of knowing when that second cup was placed down on the coaster at the side of the chair. No sooner would I open the morning paper than I would hear the thud of two feet hitting the ground from the great height of a double bed. For someone so petite she had the impact on an upstairs floor akin to that of a herd of elephants. By the time the first headline was being read she would be shouting from the top of the stairs.

"Bacon, eggs, black." would warble down the stair before a door shutting as she went to her morning routine.

Bacon and egg are self-explanatory, black was the expression of desire for a black coffee. Sometimes it was white, sometimes froth (cappuccino) and occasionally orange juice. Black was the demand before a long day, as if the addition of milk may somehow diminish the potency of the caffeine.

I prepare the food dutifully as a good father, or servant, should. Being a single father to girls means it is sometimes hard to distinguish between your role of protector, mentor, guide, and servant. Their mother left while they were both relatively young and I found my role as primary care giver expand. This required me to learn more about makeup and hair that I ever thought I would need to. At least for Sarah's purpose, her older sister was much more independent and stronger willed. I rarely needed to make her breakfast anymore.

After bouncing downstairs as beautiful as ever Sarah consumed her breakfast as if food was a growing scarcity. For someone with such a slight frame her appetite had never been anything more than gluttonous. The only explanation I can give for her lack of horizontal growth was her energy. She was more alike to the Roadrunner than anyone I had ever met. Always on the move and always full of the joys of spring, Sarah never stopped. She rarely slept more than six hours a night and was never too tired to get involved in life. No sooner had she eaten than she vanished once more, sprinting up the stairs and banged about as if she was knocking walls down. She sprung downstairs, ever the happy gazelle, this time with her rucksack over her shoulder. Although she was only going camping for a few days she had a rucksack with enough space to pack for the ascent of Everest. At least there was enough space until she filled it with only God knows what. She would call them essentials, and over the years I learned that our views on what I considered essential and what my daughter did were wildly opposing.

I threw her backpack into the car and the two of us buckled in and headed off on what, unbeknownst to us, would be our last journey together. Sarah was a huge music fan, and she insisted on controlling what was played in the car. She usually got her way, mostly because her approach was sweet therefor never came across as brattish or controlling. She was an intelligent young lady and could run logical rings round most people. In cases such as the 'car tunes', as she called them, the finale was always the same; a perfectly rational and well thought out argument as to why she should be the one that decides what is listened to. On his trip it was a particular blessing as she sang along to what she called music. Personally, the noise was to me more like repetitive torture, but she was enjoying it and it took my mind off the real issue. The trip.

This was the first time Sarah had been away with a mixed gender group. Although a young woman she was to me still a little girl and I worried about such things. I was not naïve enough to think there had not been boyfriends in the past, although I had met none. A camping trip in a remote area with a group of boys, however, was not something any father would look forward too. She had earned the right to make her own decisions and for me to trust in them. That did not negate that it is a father's job to worry. She knew this and had gone to extra lengths to try and make me feel more comfortable.

"'Don't worry dad, there are other girls there." she would tell me, as though that offered any semblance of reassurance.

While my brain would be telling me 'Yes but none of them are as beautiful as you' my mouth would be saying 'oh, that's good'. In this instance her beautiful, if out of tune, singing was helping me avoid the myriad of scenarios my brain would try and force on me. It seems somewhat ironic now that none of those scenarios came close to the reality of the situation.

The train station was not far from the house, so it did not take us long to arrive there. As there were fifteen minutes until the train was to arrive, we both went inside. We grabbed a quick coffee and sat chatting about nothing in particular. I reminded her to look after herself, which was my way of saying 'watch the boys' and she told me about the latest goings on in her world, which consisted of the occasional glance at the phone between stories of University and the latest news in what was wrong with the world. Sarah's energy often lured people into a false sense of security about her intelligence. They did not realise until in conversation that she was one of the brightest people they would meet. Her friendly and bubbly demeanour would put you at ease and make it difficult to disagree with her. She would passionately and empathically explain the ills of a world which, in her eyes, had left less fortunate people behind. Sarah always had a cause. It was never merely for the sake of conversation. Her beliefs were deeply held, and she fully engaged in trying to solve issues rather than just pontificate about them.

As always, she had me wrapped around her little finger when the train arrived, and she sprang up to make her way to the platform. A swift kiss on the cheek and a parting sentence.

"I love you dad, don't worry. I will see you soon."

These were the last words she ever said to me, the last time I ever heard her voice. Had I known that I would have recorded it, to play it back time after time after time. Instead I locked it away in my heart and used it as a whip with which to flog myself every time I realised that I had failed her.

Away she went and I returned to my car to make the short journey home. The worry had not left me even though I knew everyone in the group she was spending the weekend with. I also knew their parents which was of more importance than knowing the youngsters themselves. I was somewhat mollified by this, as well as by the fact that her first time away with a group of others was not to a debauched party destination likely to turn up on a lurid television show. The group were, at least on the surface, a sensible bunch of young adults who would likely make good decisions. Good being relative when measured against what media had shown us in recent years.

Arriving home, I busied myself as best I could. Sarah had prepared me for the fact that phone signal was likely to be weak in the camping area. I knew where she would be, with whom and for how long. I also knew it was a four-hour train, or six-hour drive, from the house. That gave me an approximation of the time by which we would lose contact, although I was sure that upon arriving in the local village they would go to a local pub for a drink before heading to their campsite.

A multitude of times since that day I have asked myself what would have happened had I researched the area they were going to. This is what I consider to be my first and greatest failing in the last ten years. Had I learnt more about the area I would have been in a position to stop Sarah from going camping. I would have been able to save my daughter's life.

I did not research though, ineptitude at its greatest depth, and accepted that my daughter knew what she was doing. Her level of maturity was of that far greater than her peers, so I foolishly thought she was fully knowledgeable about the area to which she was travelling.

It has been suggested by some that Sarah and her friends had researched the area. That the legends surrounding the Redwood forest was a lure for young adults looking for some excitement and a story to return with. While I could believe this of her friends, I cannot believe someone as savvy as Sarah would risk such a trip. A few hours into her journey Sarah sent me message.

'All is good' it read, 'will text you when we arrive'.

I was always one to prefer a phone call than a text message however Sarah was constantly texting. Her fingers moved at an unfathomable speed as I watched, usually with a mix of amazement and horror. To me the art of communication was dying in front of my eyes however Sarah assured me this was a generational thing. I was old, apparently, and technology was changing at a pace such geriatrics as myself could not keep up.

A few hours later came the final message.

'Arrived safe, heading to the campsite now'.

That was the last thing my daughter ever communicated to me. Many events surrounding this break my heart, but few more so than the knowledge that she thought she was safe as she headed into the woods with her friends.

I spent the next few days worried what she and her friends may be getting up to, youngsters with freedom, alcohol, and cold nights encouraging the sharing of bodily warmth. It seems strange to think now that I would consider a return of those days to be three days of bliss. I would do anything for that level of worry again. At the time it seemed so much but I have come to realise it was normal. I have not known normal since.

# CHAPTER 2

Local legends are complex and unusual stories. Depending on whom you engage with you will hear different flavours of the local tale. There are common strands of story amongst the various yarns, enough to be sure that each version of the legend refers to the same story. Where there is commonly divergence in detail it appears to be amendments or embellishments passed through time and regional variance. The legend of the original Redwood Massacre is no different. It has a central, core aspect which underpins the rest of the legend, whichever version you choose to believe.

The undeniable fulcrum of this legend is the actions of an unnamed local farmer, who went from loving husband to axe wielding psychopath in the seeming blink of an eye.

It was July 1972, an unusually hot and humid summer for the area. Farms were struggling because of the lack of moisture usually brought by summer showers. This one farm was not immune to the pressures. It struggled with its crops and keeping the livestock watered and fed. There is no doubt that this stress would mount unbearable pressure on even the most experienced of farmers. While nowadays it is not uncommon to see a farmer driving a nice Range Rover, or something similar, the Seventies were a different time. Most farms were small holdings and struggled to make ends meet year after year. They lived hand to mouth and the farmer, usually the father at that time, would be working fifteen-hour days just to put food on the table.

The farm was located in a remote area. It sat on the edge of a large Redwood forest covering over forty-six square miles, itself sitting in a mountainous region spanning one hundred and fifty square miles. The Redwood forest is constant contradiction. At times it is dark and dense, with a sense of foreboding as you trek through with the daylight being choked by the thick branches above. In other areas it opens to let stream and rivers flow through, creating corridors of bright sunlight and a lush green canopy which is dotted with purple heather in the summer. You glide from claustrophobia to agoraphobia without realisation. It would be the perfect hunting ground for any monster in any story but would also be the perfect setting for romance and passion.

I shall not name where this forest lies. This is not out of respect for the locals but to stop the curious from visiting and adding to the numbers of the missing. Contributing to the lack of concrete facts about what happened was the reality that residents, including the police and newspapers, were not keen on such grotesque stories being published about the area. This motivated them to write a short story about a local farmer and his family dying in the summer of '72 through unknown means. It was posited in the papers that the heat played a factor, as though it was believable that a family would allow itself to die from heatstroke or dehydration in such a modern age. It suited the residents to keep the truth hidden, a dirty secret which would haunt them for almost fifty years.

Through my investigations into what happened I can reveal for the very first time the truth of the original massacre. During the course of my research I made contact with one of the original investigating police officers. He was young and green at the time so followed his superiors' lead without question. Being a smart and ambitious young man, he kept thorough notes on the progress and findings of their inquiry. I spoke with him at length and he shared his notes with me, which I have verified through combinations of newspaper clippings, local stories and carbon dating the paper on which the notes were taken.

# CHAPTER 3

What follows is the truth of what happened that summer in 1972, revealed as fact for the very first time.

The summer was indeed one of the driest and hottest on record. The Farmer, as he is known in the notes, was struggling to not only keep his crops growing but was out in exposed sunlight and heat for between twelve and fifteen hours a day. The dry weather had an impact on the spring which fed water into the family home, a small cottage with two bedrooms. Sitting on the edge of the Redwood forest, the cottage was modest but comfortable. Living with the Farmer was his wife, whom he had been married to for twelve years, and their two children. Working the fields all day the Farmer spent his spare time chopping wood in preparation for the winter. This was, it seems, common practice in those days. During the driest weather, the wood was chopped and left in a location with good sun exposure to continue drying out. For most this would have been physically impossible, however the Farmer was documented as being a large, muscular man standing at around six feet and seven inches. Such physical exertion created a man capable of wielding an axe with devastating power.

What drove the Farmer to take the actions he took no-one will ever know. The area already had a legend of the Bodach who would take the form of a scarecrow to torment men until they went crazy. This centuries old legend was no doubt based on historical misunderstandings of what we now know to be mental health conditions. It is known that by treating mentally ill patients as criminals it exacerbates their condition and, in a small select few, can contribute to an escalation into vicious violence.

The known outcome of his turn to violence was the massacre of his entire family. Or, at least, the suspected massacre of his entire family.

It appears that the first murdered was his wife. Her mutilated remains were found in a shallow grave, alongside two other graves. From what could be extrapolated from the remains, she had been murdered using the Farmers axe. The level of brutality and degree of physical damage sustained by the wife led the investigating team to deduce that the attack had to have been perpetrated by a tall and strong individual. The axe was found with human tissue still on it, beside the Farmers body. He had hung himself on the thickest branch on the thickest tree at the edge of the Redwood forest.

His hanging corpse wore the mask of a scarecrow. A hideous piece of attire, the scarecrow mask was designed and made to terrify the birds from the field. By all descriptions, the mask would terrify any living being who came across it. Documented as being made from a thick burlap sack with sown over the eye sockets it covered the farmers' entire head. This created a menacing and featureless face, neither displaying pleasure nor distress to whomever it graced. It was an empty and emotionless face staring back at you.

Prior to his suicide he had murdered both of his children. It was deduced he had killed his wife first. The evidence supporting this theory was one of the grisliest of discoveries. In the kitchen of their cottage there was a stew of sorts, in which were parts of the Farmers wife. He had used her to create a family meal, in the most sinister of meanings. It was believed that this meal was fed to the children as there were three dishes at the table with various degrees of consumption completed. The only plate that was clear was at the head of the table, and thus assumed to the be the Farmers plate. The other two plates were partially eaten. It was suspected that the children knew they were being forced to eat their mother, or at least had a deep-rooted suspicion that this was the case. It would be unusual for children to insult their hard-working father by not eating all their meal.

Next to the mothers' grave was two others.

Both being clearly smaller in size the investigating officers had deep suspicions about what they were going to find. Two missing children, two small shallow graves. The funny thing about knowing the outcome of your investigation is that you never truly know. Such was the case in this instance. The first grave they dug up contained the mutilated body of a young girl, the daughter. She had been beheaded, the act of a truly deranged individual. Not only had he killed his own daughter, but he separated her limbs from her body in an almost ritualistic manner.

The second shallow grave contained both something and nothing. There was no body in the grave, yet there was what appeared to be a significant amount of staining from blood. By all accounts, there should have been a body housed in the grave, but there was none. Officers searched the cottage, the outbuildings and the surrounding area but could not locate the boy's body. All they found was a bloody t-shirt, a perfect fit for a child of such an age, and a child's shoe. As with the t-shirt the shoe was drenched in blood. Being that this was a time before DNA analysis could have identified the source of the blood all that was matched was the blood type. Unsurprisingly both siblings shared blood type, so this was of no actual use in resolving the mystery of whether the blood belonged to the boy.

For the officers, it seemed safe to assume the

boy was also dead. Why a grave was dug and then filled while empty was a riddle they could never solve. There were no living relatives in the area for the boy to have run to. The neighbouring farm was over half a mile away and had seen neither hide nor hair of the boy. The scene that had been found supported the theory that the Farmer had also killed his son, but for some reason had carried out something different with his body. The ritualistic nature of the murders also supported such conjecture. The consumption of the mother, the quartering of the daughter.

The boys' body was never found, and no child ever appeared matching his description.

These are the facts, according to the investigating officers. No such details have ever officially been made public, although much of the details have leaked through rumours which now form the consistent base of the Redwood Massacre legend.

Everything else, including the theory I am about to discuss, is nothing but speculation at best and complete fiction at worst.

# CHAPTER 4

The most prevalent theory, or legend, is that of the Bodach. In Celtic cultures the Bodach is a particularly nasty spirit. The Bodach tricks his victims through manufactured premonitions and visions, driving their subject crazy in the process. The reason that this particular theory has gained so much traction is because there is an even older legend passed down through generations of the 'Redwood Bodach'.

Although most of the story has been lost over time through natural degradation of a verbally passed yarn it still has elements floating in local lore. The name 'Redwood Bodach' comes from a rough translation of some Celtic text found in one of the many caves in the area. Its exact translation is believed to be closer to 'Forest Trickster Spirit', however that does not have quite the same ring to it. In the Celtic lore the Bodach would torment anyone who stepped foot into his forest, usually leading to the unfortunate victim taking their own life. The Bodach only ever tormented men, leading some to believe its vengeful nature stemmed from some traumatic past life. Only a few strands of the legend have the Bodach convincing an otherwise peaceful person to commit acts of violence against others. Most violent incidents passed in this story were believed to be carried out by already deranged men with known histories of violence.

There are two central reasons behind the Bodach legend being the favoured tale to share amongst a group.

Firstly, the Farmer was believed to be a doting and loving husband and father. There were no local stories in which he was anything other than a wonderful individual. He barely drank and did not seem to have any carnal vices out with his marriage. As we now know mental illness can emerge at any point in a person's life and their history does not always align with the manifestation of their illness. In the Seventies however such understanding of mental illness was absent so other explanations were sought. It did not seem to matter how fantastical in nature those explanations turned out to be.

Secondly the ongoing disappearance of visitors has led to stories of a spirit, or evil presence, which haunts the forest. Whether this presence takes on the physical characteristics of the farmer or is a reincarnated reaper sent from the depths of hell are open to debate. There is even suggestion that the son haunts the forest. He is said to take his vengeance out on the innocent as retribution for the local resident's inability to protect him when he was a young innocent.

Since the initial and confirmed murder of the Farmers family, and his subsequent suicide, residents have avoided the Redwood forest. They scare their children with stories of the Bodach, of the Farmer who slaughtered his family. As gruesome and unnecessary as this would seem if taken out of context, it is no different than other tales of caution we teach our young. The wicked witch who eats children, or the troll who lives under the bridge. The local aspect of the story gives it a certain potency amongst the youth however as with all tall tales it can also have the opposite effect. Every so often rebellious teenagers will test the legend.

In the forty years leading up to Sarah's disappearance, sixty-seven people are known to have gone missing in the Redwood forest. Almost exactly half of them have come from the local village. Still there has not been a concerted effort to solve these mysteries. It is almost as though living in the village has a price, a sacrifice that some families need to make in order to keep a larger peace. The village houses just over six thousand residents. While described as a village, in reality it is closer to a collection of hamlets loosely affiliated by their location. Surrounded on three sides by the Redwood forest and on the other by a steep hill. There is one road in and therefor only one road out. The village has the amenities a village of such size would have. There were two local pubs both of which served average food and below average drinks, a shop within which is a post office, a local police station and a library. The police station was manned part time by two officers, both deemed competent by the local authorities to manage an area with such an illustrious history.

If you thought that sixty-seven missing people, thirty-five of whom are from the village itself, would warrant further investigation then you would be in good company. Many families through the decades have petitioned for deeper investigations, or a government enquiry. With no bodies or evidence of violence these pleas have fallen on deaf ears.

# CHAPTER 5

After the weekend passed, I waited for a call from Sarah. She was usually so reliable when it came to keeping her word that instantly I was worried. As a father you know when your worry is discomfort versus knowledge that something is wrong, and I knew something was wrong. My first act was to call Sarah's older sister, Laura.

Laura and I had a strained relationship. She was strong willed and at a young age had pushed the boundaries in a way I struggled to tolerate. The more I tightened my grip around her behaviour, the more she slipped through my fingers. Her relationship with her sister, however, was rock solid. They had been close throughout the years, despite a five-year age gap. If there had been an issue Sarah could not discuss with me, I knew she would have been in contact with Laura. I had a haunting suspicion as I dialled Laura's number that she had not heard from her sister and quickly found out my suspicions were correct. Laura had not spoken with her sister since the train journey. Panic set in quickly, although Laura tried to assure me that there was nothing to worry about yet. It was that last word 'yet' that stuck with me. Laura was never one to alarm easily but that last work gave away that she too was uncomfortable with the silence from her sister. I rushed into calling the police only to be met with the standard response.

"Sir it's been less than twenty-four hours, there's nothing we can do just now." Polite but dismissive.

I know that you can report someone missing straight away, however the police do not have to action the report immediately. They consider several factors before deciding when, and what, action to take. In Sarah's case she was young, healthy and with friends. Likely, in most people's minds, to be having too much fun to phone father. I knew differently.

I called Laura back and told her I was heading to the Redwood forest. She told me to stay put just now, but she knew I am too stubborn to listen to others. It is one of the few traits we share. She said she would 'hang fire' and meet the train Sarah was supposed to be coming in on. The time of my arrival at Redwood would be about the same time the train arrived home. Thankful for her help I packed a few overnight things and threw a bag into the car.

I wish I could say it was a calm and controlled drive, but I would be lying to both myself and you. I drove frantically, often exceeding the speed limit as I rushed North. I switched between talk radio, music, and silence as I tried to focus on the road in front of me. It was a difficult task, but I needed to keep my mind on my journey and not on the litany of misfortunes which could have befallen Sarah. It was a tortuous and stressful commute. I still remember almost every aspect of that drive. The smell of the car and the feel of the tarmac under the tyre. I had to stop once for a comfort break and coffee. The coffee was poor, closer to drinking black mould than an aromatic blend to which I was accustomed. One assumed that there was caffeine in the bitter water so it should serve its purpose. Coffee had only become a pleasure to me as I got older. In my younger years it was a necessary hot drink containing the caffeine I assumed I needed to get through studies or stressful days.

Even the poor coffee could not wrest my mind from Sarah. After all it was her who introduced me to 'coffee for pleasure'. She used to delight in finding the most obscure coffee blend until she found ones which met her cryptically high standard. She was not a 'quick coffee' person, so the drive through coffee franchises which sprang up would never meet her expectations.

I arrived at Redwood early evening and headed straight to the police station. The station was a small, old building more reminiscent of a shack than anything official. It should not have been a surprise to me. As I drove through the village it was like the time had stood still as though the seventies had never passed. The newest car parked along the street must have been at least six years old and even it was not an expensive car. It felt like every curtain twitched as I sped down the street, but that surely was my imagination. The surrounding beauty attracted many visitors to the general area. It looked as though most tourists had given this village a miss.

The streets were eerily quiet, especially as this was a summers evening. Expectation would be there would be some life, even if it were staggering locals making their way to and from the local drinking establishments. There was no sign of anyone. I later came to learn that this was common when it was established that someone had gone missing. The locals shut down, locking themselves away from the outsiders who would be questioning their tranquil corner of the world.

Apart from terraced housing, at least a hundred years old, there were newer houses which stretched into the lower hills. Spread out quite well it was clear that, as with most places, there was a wealth divide. The village had grown such that the more affluent could look down upon the lower classes. This probably stemmed from the days of the wealthy landowners looking down upon their farm hands.

In usual times I would have been intrigued by such propositions and I would try to uncover the history of the area. I am normally fascinated by how society develops in different parts of the world. Even a journey of twenty miles can reveal stark cultural and architectural differences. In this village alone culture, architecture and wealth varied so drastically it would make for fascinating research. This was not a usual time however and my focus had to remain on Sarah. Little did I know at the time how much the history and diversity of the village related to my daughter's disappearance.

The police answered their door after much encouragement. I would have stood knocking until my knuckles bled and it felt I was not far from that point before I heard the clicking of a door unlocking from the other side. What appeared before me was like something out of a poor Eighties comedy sketch. A portly police officer, mouthful of sandwich, was standing looking back at me. Although not grossly overweight he had enough additional weight around the middle to stretch his obviously too small uniform. His face was a mix of confusion and annoyance, but you could see the thought process was underway as he tried to figure out why I was there. Before I had a chance to speak the officer-initiated contact. Bits of sandwich flew forward from his mouth as he murmured.

"Just one minute, I'll be right back."

With that the door was closed again. I stood incredulous at the swift shutting of the door. I raised my hand to knock again when I heard raised voices inside the station. I could not make out the words, but they sounded stressed. I leaned forward, as if an extra inch might reduce the muffling of the words by the heavy wooden door. As I did so the door swung open and greeting me was almost the exact opposite of what came before. A tall and lean older officer stood before me. His uniform was immaculate, and he was the picture of professionalism.

"I assume you're here about the missing kids?"

This should have set alarm bells ringing. After all I had not reported them missing, not to this force anyway. The operator I spoke to when I tried to report Sarah missing took no details so there could not have been a call ahead to warn the officer of my arrival. My jaw felt like it had hit the ground. Did they know something? Had they found something?

# CHAPTER 6

Sarah had always been a shining beacon in my life. She lit me up like no one else ever could. The perfect combination of beauty and brain, Sarah was on the fast track to a brilliant life and career.

I always worried that growing up without their mother in their life would negatively impact my daughters. Although I would not change the life, we had I am without doubt that they both would have preferred a mother and father, as opposed to just their father. Selfishly I found getting to play both roles meant I was far more integrated into theirs lives than most fathers are. However, I know that, certainly with Laura, a mother's presence would only be a positive influence in their life. I could never explain fully to them why their mother left, nor why she did not stay in contact. I am not sure of the why.

Their mother was an intelligent woman but extremely strong willed. She did not suffer fools gladly, but she seemed happy and content with our life together. There was a gap between Laura and Sarah. Laura was eight when Sarah was born, and already had grown into an independent, if fiery, little lady. Sarah was barely six months old when their mother left. She does not even have the memory of her. Laura was understandably filled with anger at her mother's flight. I was the lightening rod for that anger which only grew worse over the years. She blamed me for her mother leaving. Over the years she developed the belief that somehow my insistence on high standards drove her mother away.

There were many nights after Sarah was born that my wife would disassociate herself from her newest child. Many evenings she sat detached and emotionless. The nights she did not were filled with tears and shouting. We did not know enough about post-partum depression at the time, and the toll on our marriage was exceptionally high. We fought constantly, and I could not understand where the issues and anger were rooted. I demanded that she act the same way with Sarah as she had with Laura when she was a baby.

Hindsight is the greatest whip with which to punish ourselves. Had I known or recognised what was going on then perhaps things would have turned out differently. Laura was right in one aspect. My failure to recognise and act on my wife's depression was a large contributor to our relationship suffering and eventually breaking down. My wife did not want to seek help. When someone refuses help there is extraordinarily little you can do, you can only support in the best manner possible. It is not an easy thing and takes immense strength to support someone who is suffering so much. I was not good at this, and instead I ploughed my energy into my daughters.

The signs of my wife's impending departure were there, so I was not completely surprised the morning that the car was gone. She had not taken any clothes or personal belongings. The night before we had a massive argument, and I had been filled with such rage I had not felt before. The next morning, she was gone. She had not even taken her bank cards.

What surprised me was we never heard from her again. We contacted the police, and they investigated it. They found her safe and well, but she did not want to return. She told them she needed a break. That was the last we ever heard from her. We do not know where she went or whether she recovered from her illness. My daughters tried to find her several times over the years but with no success.

Playing both roles meant I was involved in almost all aspects of my daughter's lives, but far more so with Sarah. Laura always kept me at arm's length. The two were best friends, despite the age difference. This means for the things Sarah could not come to me for she always had Laura. I was thankful for this, there are certain changes young women go through that I was not ready to have to help manage. For most other things I was there.

I was the one that took them to see the "teen films" and listened to the terrible pop music. I was there to wipe the tears after someone had been verbally destructive. I did the bake sales, although I have to confess, I bought from a local bakers and passed them off as my own.

My presence in Sarah's life in such a way meant she was driven to success in a way that Laura was not. Sarah would soak up knowledge like a sponge and looked to me to guide and mentor her in how the world works. Her insatiable thirst for information led to her sailing through school, passing most classes with ease and giving herself the choice of further education. University was a non-negotiable for me. After Laura's failure to apply herself academically meant she bypassed university I was not going to make the same mistake with Sarah. Everything was planned out, and from an early age I identified three schools which would be acceptable places of study. We then worked over the years to attain the goal of admittance. Unsurprisingly Sarah had the pick of all three when the time came.

Sarah was highly intelligent and driven, however she was not what could be considered a nerd. Although she was studious and focussed, she was also very athletic. She competed regionally in athletics and was successful at various disciplines. The combination of intelligence and athletic prowess meant she was a popular girl at school. Sarah had a large and diverse group of friends. Unlike the popular kids you see at school Sarah had friends in her group who were not particularly attractive or were overweight. These flaws did not matter to Sarah who always saw the person inside.

There were boys, of course. Sarah was beautiful, with her long dark hair and welcoming smile. It was always understood that the rules around boys would be adhered to, that anything else was not acceptable under my roof. Curfews were important, as was meeting the boy before any dating. This was the only area Sarah and I did not see eye to eye, however she respected me enough to follow my lead on the issues. We argued sometimes about her perceived lack of freedom and I would often remind her of what I was providing for the family. For such provision to continue I must have peace of mind, and that is achieved through rules. I have no doubt that when she left for university, she was glad to be free of such sensible demands but I believe that the core principles remained with her.

After he success at school it was only natural that she would choose an important course which would lead to a career in something that matters. I always liked the idea of Sarah becoming a lawyer, but her empathy and compassion meant that was unlikely. Sarah chose medicine and started her road to becoming a doctor. I couldn't have been prouder. My daughter was going to the best university in the country to study medicine.

Sarah completed her first year with ease and was ready to start her second year. She never got the chance. She was nineteen years old when she went camping in the Redwood forest.

# CHAPTER 7

I entered the police station behind the older officer. He sat me down and instructed the younger officer to fetch me a cup of tea. Even given the situation I tried to remain polite and calm. I was always of the opinion if you keep on the good side of authoritative figures you are more likely to get the help or result you seek. I allowed them to fritter time away, as I knew in the long run my accommodating demeaner would work to my advantage. The older officer sat down and started to talk to me, explaining how they knew the reason for my visit.

It seems that the police in this village have their eyes on everything and were well aware of the visitors arriving at the weekend. As a welcoming, they often approach younger groups of tourists to make sure behaviour expectations are set. Do not drink too much. No unmanaged fires in the forest. Respect the local community. This was not unheard of in small villages around the area. Suspicion of urbanites is rife in the backwater abodes which litter the country. He assured me the group had been polite and respectful. There had been no trouble before they headed to the woods. I showed the officer my daughters' picture on my phone. I needed to make sure we were talking about the same group.

"'Yep, she was one of the youngsters. Sparkly young thing she was."

'She was'. That stuck with me, as though somehow a weekend in the woods would remove the sparkle from someone so young. The officer continued to explain that their car was still at the woods parking area, just a few miles from the village. Officers often patrolled the area, he told me, as it is a popular spot for local youths and their illicitly procured alcohol.

"They probably just extended their weekend, they'll appear tomorrow." The officer supposed.

It seemed it was not uncommon for people to extend their stay. As an area of natural beauty visitors were often awestruck by what they experienced and wanted to capture an extra day of tranquillity. Or so the officer wanted me to believe. My daughter is not most people. I know she would not take such an action without letting me know first.

I told the officer I was going to head up to the car park. His face turned ashen.

"No sir, now I wouldn't be doing that." he lectured.

There was no stopping me however, so I pressed my point. My daughter was missing, and I was not going to sit on the side lines letting precious time slip away. It was at this point I got my first glimpse of the fear that gripped the village. The older office insisted that they take me up and back and stay with me, especially as dusk was approaching.

"Easy to get lost if unprepared." he told me.

The look on the younger officers' face told a different story. It read of a man who did not want to go near the forest, let alone at dusk.

"Don't worry sir, we have a thousand visitors to these woods a year and most come back without a problem."

The word most that unsettles me even to this day. It is almost as though the best you can hope for is that not everyone goes missing. I cannot imagine another police force in this country who would accept 'most' visitors surviving their area. 'Most' seems like an exceptionally low target to try and achieve.

I was escorted to the local hotel, which doubled as one of the village bars. I wondered why there would be a room free at the height of summer. I since discovered that the hotel always has one spare room for the families of people who have gone missing in the woods. I was met with a mixture of curiosity and suspicion from the locals as

I hurriedly checked into the hotel. It was a well-worn path I was treading, the anxious relative of someone who had entered the woods never to come out. The hotel owner herself was friendly to the point of inappropriate. I suspect her role was to put relatives at ease. There was no such chance with me, and this seemed to encourage her to go over the top with her act. Touching, stroking of my arm, and attempted seductive looks were showered upon me. At any other time, the attention would be appreciated. She was attractive for the area. In a more sophisticated urban setting, she would not stand out from the crowd. Where the crowd is arguably lower class, she was almost what you would consider pretty. It felt little more than a delaying or distraction tactic than a true flirt. A practiced act to take the attention of the curious or concerned.

I checked in as quickly as I could and threw the one hastily packed bag I had into the room. Managing to avoid small talk I started to make my way out. It was at this time that I became aware of every patron in the bar watching me. Eyeballs burrowing into my psyche as I weaved my way between tables and out through the front entrance, eager to get moving with the police. I will never forget that feeling. I have never felt so unwelcome before. The unease was a warning of what was to come. This was a village that welcomed outsiders only when outsiders were there for pleasure.

The police car sat out front of the pub, engine running. They knew I was not going to take long, despite the obvious attempts to slow me down. I got into the back of the car. The first thing that struck me was the oddity of there not being any partition between the front and the back of the police car. This was a vehicle used post arrest to transport criminals. While I understand that an area such as this was unlikely to have many hardened offenders is still seemed strange to forego such standards. The forest parking was only a few miles from the village, but the drive seemed an eternity. In part this was because of my anxiety and desperation. The other factor was the poor quality of the road. Not only was it almost nauseatingly winding but the surface was a mix of broken tarmac and gravel. The car jerked and bumped as we drove between twenty and thirty miles an hour, taking more than ten minutes to get to the forest entrance. As we arrived, I could already see a parked 2003 Range Rover matching the description Sarah had given of her friend's car. Beside it sat a smaller car, probably that of her other friends. As we got closer, I could see it was a Fiat 500. This was a car preferred by younger women due to its 'quirky' design. The police car parked close and I quickly got out and moved toward the Range Rover. The officers were warning me of something, but I was not in the mood for listening. I reached the cars and checked the Range Rover first. Trying the doors was of no use, the car was still locked. I cupped me hands around my eyes and peered into the passenger side window. There were no signs of any camping equipment or personal belongings, ignoring the empty coffee cup.

I turned and moved toward the Fiat 500. The police were moving slowly toward me yelling something about contamination, but I did not listen. I tried the Fiat driver's side door and it opened. This was typical I thought to myself. Sarah was always leaving the car unlocked, as if it were somewhere in the female gene to do so. Over the years I have learned to scold myself for such casual misogyny. I sat in the driver's seat and popped open the glove box, as if it would magically contain a note or clue as to what was happening. Nothing of any importance. A few napkins most likely from a fast-food drive through and some bobby pins.

It is nothing short of amazing how the mind works. Bobby pins brought a smile to my face. As a father of two daughters I spent my life finding bobby pins littered throughout the house, the car and even the garden. At one point I became sure that they were multiplying. Perhaps like Mogwai they multiplied when wet. No matter how many I picked up and either binned or put back into the bathroom, moments later there were always more. Not until I grew my hair longer did I appreciate their power and importance. Sarah was usually the main culprit behind the bobby pin invasion. Laura was far more disciplined in almost every way.

My momentary mental break was disturbed as the older officer reached the car door and leaning on it with one arm I finally heard what he had been shouting.

"If anything did happen to this group, you have now contaminated the entire scene. Anything found would be useless now."

I took him at his word, not realising that in the world of forensics his statement was, in essence, bullshit. At the time I knew no better so I got out of the car and did not touch anything else. I wandered a few meters from each car looking to see if anything had been dropped or marked that would indicate the direction in which they went. There were no official paths through these woods, however there were various routes into the trees. It was at this point I finally looked up at the forest.

The Redwood forest is a daunting wall of wood. As expected, it is filled with large redwood tress however there was a mix of other large trees intertwined throughout the forest. It struck me as strange that such a mix of tree species would be so mingled together. I had never seen such a combination of natural and unmanaged growth. It created a formidable wall of green, in some ways unwelcoming due to the sheer height of the trees.

In other ways this was an intriguing and inviting mystery. The wood was so thick that where there are gaps to enter the forest you could not see anything but more trees. It draws you in. Behind the wall of green are mountains, hills, and rivers. There are areas of open space speckled throughout the forest. This makes it even more appealing, as if there is some secret magical land just beyond the thicket of towering lumber. I turned to the officers looking for guidance on what path to the campsite.

"Campsite?" said the younger officer. "No campsites in there, not officially. Campers enter at their own risk."

Risk? Why would there be risk in camping in a forest in the middle of the summer, bar an accident or getting lost. It was an odd choice of words but as I was quickly learning the language used was often the veneer of normality slipping. It frequently betrayed the local's true concerns about what lay beyond.

I chose a path and started moving. The officers suddenly stopped me. My attire, the time of day and my lack of equipment meant that going into the forest at this time, just before the darkness of night starts to settle, was dangerous. I searched my thoughts. What dangers could be lurking in a forest?

Surprisingly, logic started to set in as I moved

from emotional to practical. If you are suitably prepared, then getting lost in a forest such as this should pose no dangers. The correct footwear and attire, camping equipment and food should see you right for a few days at least. I had none of these things. Although pleasantly warm during the day at night, once the sun sets, the temperature drops significantly. It would not be a pleasant night and while hypothermia would be unlikely becoming ill would be a distinct possibility.

The Redwood forests thickness in parts means only partial sunlight reaches the forest floor even on the nicest of summer days. Finding anything in the forest would be difficult in the best conditions, but completely impossible in the darkness of night.

With regret and disappointment, as well as an ever-increasing anxiety in the pit of my stomach, we headed back to the village.

Entering the hotel was eerily similar to leaving it. Almost all conversation stopped, almost all eyes moved in my direction. The little amount of chatter that continued was coming from one corner. The group excitedly talking were obviously not locals. Three men, two in expensive looking clothing fresh out of an adventure store and one dressed in more well-worn apparel. Once they realised that everyone else had stopped speaking, they quickly quietened. I was not hungry nor particularly thirsty. Nevertheless, I realised my consumption of solids and liquids that days had been foolishly low. It made sense to find a spot and order some food with something to drink. Usually I am sensible about my nutrition. I have always cared about being in good shape and healthy and eating too little can be as damaging as eating too much. Today there was just too much on my mind. I found a small table as far from everyone else as one could get in such a confined space. The chair was, of course, wobbly. It was the sort of pub where you would see such minor issues resolved by a beer mat being placed under the leg of a chair or table. Unfortunately, I could not even see beer mats, just stained sticky tables.

I picked up the sparse menu that sat proudly on the table. Typical fare for the area. I went for something meaty with vegetables. What came was close to meat, although I am not sure either which animal it was from or what part of the animal it was from. Almost passable food washed down by unpleasant local beer. I had the choice of wine, beer, or whisky. The wine looked like something that was bargain basement thirty years prior and whisky has never sat well with me. With the explosion of micro-breweries in the area I thought the beer would be a safe bet. I was quickly learning in this area there was no such thing.

I sat there for around forty minutes. In most small villages staff and patrons would happily engage in small talk. I was finding that already I was a pariah. My suspicion that this was due to the nature of my visit was reinforced by the warm welcome the three other visitors were receiving. I overheard them saying they were going into the forest the next day, hiking along a river before camping near some derelict farmhouses. I was going to engage them about my missing daughter, ask them to keep their eyes open. Looking around the room however I thought better of it. I had visions of being tossed to the street and being told to stay on the road, avoid the moors.

# CHAPTER 8

I barely slept through the night. Cell phone reception was spotty at best in the area and the hotel did not have wi-fi. I never decided if this was to ensure the tranquillity of the area or because the village was a backwater stuck in the past. Reception was good enough for text messages however and I could communicate with Laura. Sarah had not returned on the train, just as I had predicted. I was restless all night, trying to calm myself with the knowledge that the most likely situation being the group had gotten themselves lost in the forest. In this likely scenario they would safe, if a little cold and hungry. I had to stop myself from letting my mind wander toward more worrying thoughts. Had there been an accident? Had one of the group drunk too much, or worse taken something illegal and become hostile or even violent? Had they been a victim of some sort of crime? My mind came up with a plethora of scenarios, none of which even came close to the likely reality.

As soon as the sun rose, I followed. Quickly

readying myself I went downstairs. I was no better prepared than the night before. In my rush to leave the house I had not picked up any suitable footwear. During the daylight my clothing would suffice, but sneakers would just not cut it on a moss-covered forest floor littered with downed branches and leaves. There was no-one at reception. Given it was so early, and given the local nature of the hotel, this did not surprise me. An area that caters to walkers and campers should expect early rising guests, but this was not your normal village. They did not cater for visitors; visitors had to fit in to the village. The door out was open, a trusting sign of days gone by. Certainly not something you would see now in most towns and cities. Perhaps there was nothing worth stealing, or perhaps the penalty for criminality in such a small area was worse than any court would dish out.

I jumped in my car and sped over to the police station. I do not know why I didn't foresee that the officer would not be up yet. In hindsight it was an obvious turn of events. I stood blankly staring at the door.

"Ten o'clock." came a voice behind me. "They usually arrive about ten o'clock."

I turned to see an older gentleman across the read. In one hand he had an old, gnarled walking stick, likely handmade, and in the other a lead with a dog attached which looked almost as old as he did. This felt like the first sincere interaction I had with anyone in town. I took the opportunity to try and talk to him. Any engagement with a local had to be a good thing.

"I'm looking for my daughter." I explained, before giving a brief summary of the prior day's events. He looked at me with a great sadness in his eyes and pain in his face.

"Not my business to speculate. I can only wish you luck."

With that he continued walking. I tried to call to him, to keep him talking. He never turned round.

"Sorry."

That was all he said as he continued. I had never come across a place where people seemed so reticent to talk. He did not seem scared to speak. He just looked sad, almost defeated. Whatever secret this village had was a heavy weight carried by its residents. They either could not or would not talk about it.

I was not going to wait another four hours for the police to show up. I needed to start searching. If I was searching alone, so be it.

I drove the road faster than I should have. I thought I had paid particular attention the evening before, but it had become obvious my mind had been wondering. As I approached a particularly sharp bend halfway toward the forest, I hit a large hole, which can best be described as a crater. Being that I was travelling far too fast for the condition the road my tyre blew out instantly. I lost control of the car, my reactions not being quick enough to keep up with the events unfolding. There was no chance I was going to be able to navigate the bend in the road. I applied as much pressure as I could to the brakes. It was too late. In the two seconds it took for my brain to register the incident and move my foot to the brakes the car had carried on straight as the road curved left. I hit a large redwood tree head on at nearly forty miles an hour. Thankfully, the combination of a well-built car, seatbelt and airbag saved me from what would have certainly been debilitating injury. However, they could not save me from all injury.

Everything in front of me was blurry as I opened my eyes. I could taste iron in my mouth and my face felt wet. I took a few moments to gather my thoughts.

"It's not raining."

I was speaking to myself, waiting for my senses to kick in. Then suddenly pain. Shooting pain across my right shoulder. The blurriness cleared and I could see the crumpled hood of the car in front of me through a cracked and partially removed windscreen. The taste in my mouth was my own blood. My immediate concern was where was the blood coming from? The wetness on my face, on a day without rain, informed me I was bleeding externally. This was most likely from my upper head somewhere. I managed to open the car door. Thankfully, the accident had not trapped me in my vehicle and, although unsteady and sore, I pulled myself out. While the pain in my shoulder was excruciating my arm was not completely useless. I could still feel and move my fingers. I was not a medic, but I knew it was most likely a dislocation of the shoulder. My legs worked, and I seemed to be able to move around okay. There was pain in my lower back and neck, but it was not unbearable. I fumbled in my trouser pocket for my cell phone, fingers crossed that it had not fallen out in the crash. My desire to crawl about in the footwell of the car at this moment was virtually nil. Thankfully, the phone was in my pocket and I withdrew it filled with hope that someone would be called to come help. That hope quickly faded as I saw the lack of reception on the phone. This is what Sarah had told me about, there is no reception in the Redwood.

It was at this point I noticed the time. Almost two hours had passed since I set off from the village. I had sat unconscious in the car for almost two hours. When this realisation set in, I began to notice I was a little cold, and a little thirsty. It was summer, but the sun was still rising in the sky, so the temperature was on the lower side.

The bleeding would have also contributed to both the feeling of low temperature and the thirst. I was convinced that although I had not been seriously injured in the crash. I needed medical attention. That need would become greater the longer it was withheld so I had no option than to walk back to the village. I was not able to move at any great pace, so the couple of miles I had to go were going to take me at least an hour. I could only hope that my bleeding was slowing or stopping and that my battered body could keep its strength long enough to reach safety. This was a road to nowhere. The only passing vehicles would be heading for the forest, and those would be few and far between.

As I slowly made my way along the edge of the forest my mind began to play tricks on me, or at least at the time that is what I thought was happening. There were odd noises just inside the tree line, breaking branches as though some large, heavy footed creature was stalking me. It was unlikely the local deer would have a taste for human flesh, and they were the only sizable creatures in the area that I could think of. There was also a strange odour in the air, a combination of what I could only describe as rotting flesh and chemicals. At times there was a strange silhouette moving slowly in the darkness. An odd visual I can assure you, as one would not normally see movement in darkness. In this instance it was a darkening patch, as some narrow streams of light penetrated the forest canopy to create a shallow darkness. Surely with the head knock I had taken I would be carrying a concussion. These auditory and visual hallucinations were almost certainly symptoms of such a brain injury. Had I known then what I know now I would have been frozen in fear. It is testament to the expression 'ignorance is bliss'.

It did not take long for physical and mental fatigue to set in. A distance which would normally have been an early morning jog had become the equivalent of an ultra-marathon. My muscles and bones ached, and my mental fortitude had been tested already by both the accident and what I may or may not have been seeing in the forest. I stopped, having possibly only made it half a mile from the car. I began to question if I had even been going in the correct direction. Everything around me looked the same. I heard a car approaching. Another auditory illusion no doubt, and I sat down at the side of the road feeling defeated and deflated.

A giant shadow loomed over me blocking out the sunlight. I looked up and could make out no facial features, just a dark shape where a face should be. I tried to focus, squinting my eyes as I tried to make out some discerning features. The shape must have been six feet four inches or more. It almost blocked out the entire forest behind it.

# CHAPTER 9

"We need to get you up."

The voice was warm and friendly, if deep and a little gruff. He lifted me with ease, but gently as to not hurt me further. I became aware of two more human shapes, both of more normal size. The large man placed me next to the car and opened the door.

"I'm Gus." he said. "You're safe."

I made my way onto the passenger seat of the car with a little assistance from my new friend. I sat listening to him converse with his friends. They made an agreement; Gus would take me back into the village to see if there was a doctor and failing that to the nearest hospital. The hospital was a thirty-five-mile trip from the village along winding hillside roads. His friends would continue to the forest car park and wait for an hour. If Gus had not returned, they would continue with their hike and rendezvous later at the agreed camp spot. I thought rendezvous was an intriguing choice of word. Their pattern of communication had an air of formality around it, almost military in its precision. His two compatriots took their backpacks from the car and changed their footwear to something more appropriate for hiking. They said their goodbyes and Gus got into the car.

"Don't worry, we'll get you help."

It seems remarkable to think back and realise that my car crash saved Gus's life. Fate is a difficult thing to believe in even when life is going well. It is with some reticence that I put our meeting down to fate. There is little else I can put it down to, however. Had he caught up with his friends both his and my story would have been vastly different.

We drove back down to the village, with Gus very deliberately avoiding as many bumps and potholes as he could. As we arrived at the village it was still early, too early for the police station to be open. There was no obvious medical practice in the village, so Gus took me straight to the only place either of us knew, the hotel. Upon arriving Gus vanished inside and re-appeared a few moments later. He opened the door and helped me get out of the car, careful not to pull or twist me in any way as to cause me unnecessary discomfort. My overall body ache remained but my shoulder was partially numbed. I could still feel my fingers which gave me some level of comfort. It felt like the bleeding around my head had stopped, and my face now felt closer to sticky than wet.

Gus helped me inside where the hotel receptionist was waiting with a panicked look on her face. They sat me down in the bar. I was convinced if I got any sort of infection it would be from in here. I heard the receptionist tell Gus that the doctor was on his way and would be here soon. No sooner had she said that than an older gentleman arrived carrying a doctor's bag. He looked at me with fear and dread.

"Is it…" he trailed off. The receptionist looked at Gus, who looked at me, somewhat bemused.

"Is it what?" he asked. "The guys just been in a car crash." There was instant relief on both the doctors and receptionists face.

The doctor started to examine me. He mumbled something about it looking worse than it was. Directing the receptionist to get some cloths soaked in cold water he shone a light in my eyes and felt around my neck. He moved onto my shoulder at which point he lost the ability to be gentle. I flinched in pain as he prodded and twisted.

"Definitely dislocated." he muttered.

If I was looking for him to put my shoulder back into place, I was going to be disappointed. He did not look physically capable nor particularly willing.

"We need to get him to a hospital, get that shoulder reset." he proclaimed.

I protested; I did not want to waste precious time by going to the hospital. I had a missing daughter to find. I was also aware Laura would arrive at some point in the afternoon to join me. Gus offered to reset my shoulder, proclaiming expertise at such an action. The doctor declined, concerned about other damage that may have been done and not wanting to risk nerve damage. He also wanted me to get my head wound checked and tested for concussion. That seemed an unnecessary test, I was almost certainly concussed. The receptionist returned with the cloths and the doctor put them on my head, leaning me back slightly so they rested on my forehead. His logic was the cold compress would cause the blood vessels to contract which would help with bleeding and wound healing. The cold would also help me relax and numb some of the pain.

The three then proceeded to discuss calling an ambulance, which the doctor claimed would have taken at least three hours to get there.

"No problem, I'll take him." Gus was turning out to be quite my saviour.

The doctor approached me with a needle in his hand.

"For the pain." he told me.

Before I could protest, although I was in no real shape to stop him, he pushed the needle into my arm and pressed the syringe. I could feel a cold liquid enter my body. The last thing I remember is the doctor writing a short note and handing it to Gus.

I awoke feeling quite refreshed if a little sore. My pain was now more of an ache. As I opened my eyes the brightness of the room was almost blinding. It took me a few minutes for my eyes to adjust and my head started to throb as my vision began to focus. I tried sitting up, slightly unsteady and unsure of what was happening and where I was.

"Slowly." came a familiar voice beside me. I looked over and a blurred face quickly came into focus. Laura was stood next to the bed. I tried to process her presence at the hospital. How did she know where I was? How had she gotten here?

Laura was a particularly good driver who rarely drove. As part of her rebellious youth she started racing cars. Her reactions and instincts were brilliant, but she had an undisciplined and reckless streak. She was on a fast track to success when she gave it up, claiming to be bored and wanting to move onto something else. As Laura's discipline for sticking with things was poor this came as no surprise to anyone. She was brilliant but lacked focus and dedication. It was only later that we found out the death of a fellow racer had deeply affected her. She decided she did not want to race again and found driving a car normally to be extremely mundane. Which brought me back the question of how she got here?

"Evening fella." It was another familiar voice, although this time it took a few seconds to process. In the doorway stood Gus holding two cups of what I can only think contained cheap hospital coffee.

It transpired that as Gus was driving me to hospital I was talking in my semi-conscious state. I had told him or slurred like a Navy drunk as Gus would later describe it, that my daughter Laura would be arriving that afternoon and she would be looking for me. Gus had taken it upon himself to drop me at the hospital, head back to the village and wait for her. Laura would be easy to spot in the village, if not only for her out of place beauty but her confidence and, in your face, attitude. Backward villages tend to have more compliant women than the more educated areas. Gus sat in the pub awaiting a stranger's arrival, to help another stranger he had no business caring for.

Laura is suspicious of most people. Years of experience of being let down had led her to be wary of the intentions of others. I have often told her choose better friends but being headstrong she does not listen. Gus had a way of putting you at ease. For a man of his height and intimidating build one of the first things you notice is his warmth and welcoming nature. I guess when you look as though you can tear a man in half with your bare hands you gain nothing from being an asshole.

Laura took a cup from him and smiled warmly, a look I had rarely seen on her face. It seemed the two had bonded already. I would later observe a playful banter and friendly competitiveness that you would normally associate with a brother and sister. Over the years this bond would grow stronger. Gus became the big brother and protector, all whilst fighting his own guilt and demons.

I lay in the hospital bed feeling a burden of guilt. Not only was I letting Sarah down, but Gus now had further to go alone to catch up with his friends. He assured me this was not an issue. They were experienced, and he was experienced. I was not sure at this point experienced in what although I was soon to find out more. When asked what brought him to the forest his response was simple.

"I'm here to meet the bogeyman."

This was Gus's name for the Redwood legend. At this point we had not heard of the people who had gone missing over the years. Our confusion must have been obvious.

"You know, the Redwood killer?"

Still our faces were blank. The statement of a killer did not help us. We were still in the dark about the macabre history of the area.

"The Farmer?" Gus continued.

At this point it was obvious that we were oblivious. Gus sat himself down next the bed and proceeded to relay his learned version of the Redwood Massacre legend. He told the story vividly and with charisma. He clarified at the end that he did not believe a word of it, but he and his friends wanted to explore an area which could give birth to such a fantastically twisted story. They had a four-day trek with agreed rest points should anything cause them to split up. All were experienced orienteers trained in first aid and survival skills. Where these skills were learnt was still a mystery.

I had never put stock in such fiction as Gus had shared but I would be lying if at this point a cold chill did not run through my body. Laura was clearly far more sceptical than I. She scoffed at such ridiculous stories. She was a woman of the world and had seen things none of us would wish to imagine. The only common thread across the atrocities she had witnessed was they were all carried out by someone who was very human.

Gus said his goodbyes and wished us luck in the search for Laura. I hoped our paths crossed again when I felt better. I owed this man a lot. It is rare these days to find someone with such empathy for others, a true gentle giant. My wish of meeting again was granted but the circumstances of our reconnection meant it was bittersweet. Laura walked Gus out. Later if became clear why their connection was so instant, and it should have been obvious to me at the time. I was sat in a hospital bed recuperating from a car accident; my observations and intuition were not up to their usual standard.

Laura re-entered the room and proceeded to explain what had happened while I was under. They had placed my shoulder back into position without much problem and ran some tests. Concussion was a given but thankfully there were no signs of serious injury. I would be out in the morning after some rest. I protested, Sarah was now missing for almost forty-eight hours and nobody seemed concerned. If there is one thing I have always been good at it is raising a fire in Laura. Her demeanour instantly changed from concern to anger. Laura was short in stature, but she should never be taken lightly. She is as formidable a person as you will meet.

She railed at me about my attitude and selfishness. Of course, Sarah mattered to her, she had travelled up here to help search only to find her father in hospital after a car accident. She had been taught to deal with the situation closest to hand first, and that was me. I shrank back into my bed as my diminutive daughter scolded further. I was to stay put. She would head back into town now and touch base with the police. If she could catch up with Gus, she would take a ride back with him. Otherwise she would figure out alternative transportation. I was to stay put in my hospital bed. She turned to leave and, as she was halfway out of the door, she pivoted her head and looked at me with her steely gaze.

"If I see you again today, I will break enough bones to put you back into this bed for a month."

She was not joking. Although I doubted, she would injure me to that extent, she was more than capable. When it came to Laura you were sometimes better to stay out of her way. In some circumstances that worked to my advantage. I could wind her up and point her in the direction of something I needed resolved. In doing so I had to stay out of her path lest I suffer the fate I planned for others.

# CHAPTER 10

The next morning came quickly. The pain medication on offer was of the highest quality and had done its job of getting me through the night quite comfortably. It was the first full night's sleep I had had since Sarah left on her trip. Gradually the nights had been getting longer, with the climax being the previous night after seeing the edge of the forest. Not that being rested resulted in any less stress, but I certainly felt a surge of energy. I knew Laura would have already started investigating the local area and its eccentric residents. I had no doubt the police were already afraid of her. She would be asking questions they could not answer, and she is learned in interrogation techniques. Some subtle, some less so. I had to await the doctors rounds to be released from the hospital. I could have self-discharged, but Laura's warning was still ringing in my ears. Thankfully, I did not have long to wait. By ten AM I was free to leave. All I had was the blood-stained clothes I had arrived in, but they would have to do just now. My phone, wallet and watch were all beside me. I quickly text Laura. Knowing her reception would be an issue, I did not wait for a response and headed out.

I grabbed the nearest taxi which took me to a local superstore where I could get some fresh clothes. I chose quickly, not overly concerned by colour, fit or fashion. I changed into my new clothes, bagged up my soiled attire and left the superstore. Despite my request to stay, the taxi had already left so I was forced called another. After a long fifteen minute wait another taxi arrived. I got in, gave my destination, and waited to leave. The taxi did not move.

"Are you sure you want to go there mate?" the taxi driver enquired.

I let him know I was quite sure, and he shrugged his shoulders. We left the superstore and for the entire journey the driver did not say a word. All that could be heard was the noise of the road and the artificial click sound made as the trip counter passed another milestone cost.

We arrived at the village ninety minutes later. I paid the fare and I had barely gotten out of the vehicle and closed the door when the taxi hastily took off. I checked my phone. Still no response from Laura. I entered the pub through the front. It was quieter than before, there was no lunchtime rush today. I spoke to the receptionist, who during the day doubled as barmaid and waitress. She let me know Laura had been in the night before, going round different groups asking questions. I could tell be the receptionists face that she disapproved. Not that Laura would care. She usually focussed on what was necessary not what was popular. Early that morning Laura had corralled the police officers into taking her up to the forest to look around. She also managed to convince at least one local patron to donate a more suitable pair of boots and jacket for me, which were in my room. I knew that with Laura leading the effort I would do nothing but slow them down. I was still sore from the day before and would not be able to move as fast as I would like. I would focus my efforts elsewhere. Someone in this village must have been willing to talk.

I went up to my room and threw my bag of dirty clothes into the corner. Laura's bag was sitting on the chair in the corner, skilfully placed with a few items taken out and placed on the dresser. They were in perfect order. Nothing was left out of place. Hunger was creeping in. I had not dared sample the hospital food. I am sure it is never as bad as the amusing anecdotes would suggest but I did not want to take the chance. Not that the food in the pub would be much better, however I would at least have the comfort of a stronger drink to wash it down. I went downstairs into the bar area and ordered some food and a pint of their local beer. I was sure eventually I would get a taste for the bitter grain. I enquired about a local library, which I was told was only a few streets away. I assumed it would be a quiet place, the nasty part of my brain wondered how many of the residents could read. I consumed my food, which tasted as bland as before, and set off to find the library.

To my surprise the library was busier than the pub. As well as the section of computers connected to the internet there were large areas designated for sitting reading. The bookshelves were filled with various volumes of text, both fiction and non-fiction. It had the old book smell and was somewhat grand in some places. It reminded me of a library in a more cultured part of the world. It sat almost in direct opposition to the rest of the buildings I had seen. I smiled to myself as it was this library that reminded me to never judge a book by its cover. I had a history of being judgemental, and usually my first impressions were accurate. Laura would often tell me that even when I was wrong about someone, I would twist reality to suit my version of events. I reminded her that it was my approach to life that had led to my success, which enabled her to waste so many years on pointless pursuits.

The librarian sat behind an old oak desk, reading. Almost the complete stereotype. All she was missing were the reading glasses on chain around her neck. Upon request she pointed me in the direction of the news archives. Gus's story, no matter how farfetched, must have had some elements of truth to it. I found an old microfilm machine and a wall of drawers with years on them. The old local newspaper archives. Anything newer than 2005 would likely be a digital archive but this was more than enough for me to go through. I started in 1972, the year Gus had mentioned the first murders occurred. Logic dictated that murder would be front-page news in a small area like this so the narrowed down the depth of my search. If the first few pages of each edition did not mention anything I would move onto the next. I scrolled for an hour with no success. I reached the end of the year without finding a single article mentioning murder. Maybe Gus had the year wrong? Maybe the entire story was a fabrication? Almost all fiction has an element of reality to it, I reminded myself, and I was missing something. It was then that it struck me, obituaries.

Small villages do not have a high death rate, so it was unlikely that more than one full family died that year. I started searching the obituaries and it was not long before I found an obituary for a local resident, his wife and two children. There was no mention of murder, and the names had been redacted. This struck me as particularly strange, no other article in the archives for that year had been redacted. I did not have any paper or pen with me, but I had my phone. I took a note of the day and year of the deaths.

My thoughts wandered to the rest of Gus's yarn.

He mentioned over one hundred people had gone missing over the years. All were victims of the Redwood killer but there were no bodies, no sign of any crimes. The latter part I can believe. In such a large, wooded area finding forensic evidence of a crime would be near impossible. Surely though if there had been so many murders there would be bodies, or at the very least a large-scale police investigation.

The questions kept gnawing at me. What was going on here. Searching the archives for stories on missing people over a forty-year period was never going to be practical. It was the proverbial needle in a haystack. Thank goodness for the wonder of the internet, and in particular the internet connections in the library. Luckily, there was a terminal free, so I moved over to the computer and sat down. The computer was not what you would consider particularly new or advanced, and the internet connection was slow at best, but this was certainly a better option than searching microfilm archives. Not that I was completely done with those archives, however I needed more focused dates to search. I opened the web browser, accessed the best search engine I knew and typed. 'Redwood killer'. There were thousands of results.

# CHAPTER 11

The first site I listed in the search engine was titled 'The Redwood Massacre'. I clicked and was met by a gaudy website with cheap red type for the title. It was sensationalist at best, however on the surface it seemed to have a lot of information. I started reading through the various articles. Firstly, the history of the farmer whose identity had been so carefully hidden. The site did not name him, it referred to him more as a character whose real identity was masked, much like Jack the Ripper. Then various articles about missing people who entered the forest never to be seen again. I could not confirm there were over a hundred as Gus had claimed but there were more than a few handfuls. I noted down dates on my phone. The articles on the website contained no citations so I would need to verify what I was reading. For the two hours of researching I almost forgot about Sarah, and about Laura being out there near the forest.

I made my way back to the hotel hoping that Laura had returned or at least had left a message for me to pick up. Arriving back, I was met by the same receptionist she seemed to work almost twenty-four hours a day. I enquired about messages and was told there are none. I checked my phone again there was still nothing from Laura. I could feel the onset panic and the rhythm of my breath had increased. I could feel the pace of my heart increasing and at times felt like it was skipping a beat. I had no car to take me back up to the forest and I doubted if anybody in the village was going to help me. Just as I could feel the panic deepening my phone beeped twice. It was Laura.

'Just on our way back' read the text message on my phone.

I knew she could not have been far if she was getting a reception on her phone. I had the option of texting her or waiting the short period of time it would take for her to arrive back at the hotel. I decided the sensible thing would to do was wait. I felt so useless at this point; my gut was telling me to text, my head was telling me not to. It was a short wait for Laura to return. I occupied those ten minutes with a beer at the bar. I was not able to drive nor, did I have a car, so I did not see the issue in having a drink. As I sat the thoughts of the Redwood killer filled my brain. Was it possible that such a legend could be true? The logical part of my brain told me that it was nonsense. My gut on the other hand had an uneasy feeling. Laura was now missing for forty-eight hours, twenty-four of which I had spent in a hospital bed. The aches in my body were less now than before however the pain was still noticeable. I left the hospital with a handful of painkillers, but these would only impair my judgement and my intellect.

Laura strode into the pub; I could immediately tell that she was not in a good mood. She was never particularly good at hiding her emotions, she wore them on her sleeve like a badge of honour. At times it was a strength that I admired and at other times I thought it a weakness to be avoided. In this moment it felt like it was a weakness.

"Fucking imbeciles." Laura proclaimed loudly and in front of everybody.

Behind her walked two sheepish looking police officers. It was obvious it was them to which she was referring. I do not think she cared; in fact, I know she did not. She approached the table at which I was sitting. Normally I would rise to meet her but the pain in my legs told me I was better to stay seated. I looked up at her expecting her sit down. She was clearly too agitated to stay still. She looked down at me and repeated.

"Fucking imbeciles."

As she stood there, she related the day's events to me. She had 'encouraged' the police officers to rise early and head up to the forests with her at near dawn. When they arrived at the car park there were three cars now there. Two of the cars from the previous day which I had foolishly inspected against the officers wishes. The third car belonged to Good Samaritan and my saviour Gus. There is no one else around and Laura inspected both cars against the protests of the police officers. Laura was more familiar with the ins and outs of law enforcement than I was. She was perfectly aware that there was nothing wrong with inspecting the scene before a forensic team arrived. She questioned the officer's motives in trying to stop her from finding any evidence of recent activity. She reminded them that only when it is determined that a crime was committed would seal off the crime scene to stop cross contamination of evidence. It was at this point the police officers realised who they were dealing with.

Laura then 'encouraged' the officers into the forest. They had been reticent to do so and displayed fear that you would not think natural of officers of the law. A forest in most regards is nothing to be afraid of. Yet everybody I have met so far showed fear of the Redwood forest. As they were not carrying the necessary equipment, they were not able to go far into the forest and were not even sure that they were going in the right direction. They pushed on following what little evidence of tracks there were. Laura was quite aware that those tracks may have belonged to Gus and his friends. Indeed, they were the only participants of any activities in the forest out with my daughter and her group of friends. As she followed the tracks the officers behind her got further and further away. They moved with a slower and more deliberate pace, checking their surroundings as they took each considered step. Laura knew that she could not go far into the forest without the right equipment. She had let me know her disappointment that the police were not prepared for this search after forty-eight hours had passed. They found nothing in their quick search of the entrance of the forest.

I could see the concern on Laura's face. She did not shake easy, however with Sarah missing she was beginning to panic also. She looked towards the officers then back to me. I could see she was thinking, and I knew said the officers the receptionist through nobody liked what Laura said next.

"We need to pull together a search party and we need to do it now."

The officers and the receptionist looked at each other. The receptionist approached the officers and they started to mutter amongst themselves. The officers nodded and left the pub. The receptionist let us know they were going to round up a group of locals who knew the area well. She assured us that some villagers would take part, although we should not expect a large turnout.

"The forest is not a place that locals want to be."

the receptionist told us. "There's too much history."

This was the first mention that anybody in the village made to me about the forest. So many had refused to engage. Many would not even look me in the eye. I asked if it was because of the Redwood killer. She looked at me in abject horror and the colour drained from her face. He was just a story and not to be talked of. If I were to mention him again, I would get no help from the village. This set me back somewhat. It was obvious there were secrets in the village and the legend of the Redwood killer was central among them. How true the legend was we were yet to find out. What was becoming clear was that the village believed there was something evil in the hills. A darkness contained within the forest that not even sunlight could penetrate. It was as if the forest was hell itself and the devil was claiming the souls of all who entered.

It was later in the evening when a group of eight young men joined us. The youngest of the group was in his late teenage years the oldest no more than forty. The officers let us know that this was the group that had volunteered to search the forest the next day with us. He had all the equipment necessary including camping gear if we wanted to stay through the night. It struck me as odd in a village of six thousand residents that only eight would help find a missing girl. My experiences since this day have told me that getting as many as eight volunteers was, in itself, a miracle.

One of the volunteers knew the forest better than most. He introduced himself as Damien. He had not been born in the village but had lived there for the last several years. He paid no heed to the warnings or the stories of the Redwood killer. Damien was drawn to the forest by the legend of the bogeyman and he led several groups of campers through the forest all without incident. Despite never coming across any crazed killer farmers, Damien always felt an uneasy presence from the forest. He was aware of the people who went missing in the forest over the years but himself had never seen any evidence of foul play. For him this added to the intrigue and mystery and drew him deeper into the forest with each trip.

Damien identified the three most popular paths for campers and hikers took through the forest. Including the officers there were twelve of us. We were to split into three groups, meaning four of us per path. If there was anything lurking in the forest, we would have safety in numbers. It was agreed that myself and the older officer would lead one group. Damien would lead another group and Laura and the younger officer would lead the third group. There was an uneasiness with some in the group about spending the night in the forest. Laura, ever the master manipulator, challenged their masculinity by implying if a girl were to stay the night in the forest and a man would not then he was more of a boy than a man. In a village where traditional gender roles were still the norm, such a gauntlet laid down at the feet of a man's masculinity was like to a red rag to a bull. Whether these men wanted to stay in the forest or not that night they were going to.

Sarah and her friends were supposed to spend two nights in the forest. It was agreed with a more experienced group of hikers like us two days should suffice. We would be able to cover as much ground as Sarah and her friends could have in three days.

While two days still feels short to me the logic used to determine the initial search could not be argued with. We were to set off shortly after dawn, there was not much could be done before then. The eight volunteers would look after the equipment ensuring that we had all that we needed. I knew regardless of how well Laura's equipment was packed she would repack it herself. She was meticulous and exact in this way. The receptionist advised there was a separate room set up for Laura and there would be no charge for this for the next few days. While a nice gesture I could not help but think that this was made from guilt. I felt compelled to buy the group a drink and ordered beers for everybody. There was only going to be one drink that night, I wanted everybody to be bright and alert when dawn came. There was little conversation as everybody drank the bitter ale that was in front of them. Polite good nights were shared, and the volunteers left to prepare for the morning's departure. I could see that Laura was still upset with the wasted day with the police officers but there was nothing that could be done about that now. It was better to release the frustration and start again tomorrow.

There was nothing I was going to be able to do to calm her anger. I learned a long time ago that when Laura gets angry, I am fuel to the flame. In many ways we are alike and in many ways we are different. It is where we are the same that causes the most conflict. Laura is a better person than I could ever be, but I learned from my mistakes with her and did not do the same with Sarah. Therefore my connection with Sarah was different than that with Laura. I love both my daughters very much. The differences between Laura and I did not mean I love her any less than Sarah. We are simply different people with different ideals. Laura will readily point out that this is because she did not take the path I laid before her, nor meet the expectations that I had of her. I cannot argue that this is untrue but that does not mean that I was ever wrong.

# CHAPTER 12

Dawn arrived faster than I had expected. I arose, barely rested, and threw myself in the shower to try and freshen myself. The aches in my body had subsided somewhat but I knew it would not last long. We would be the slower of the groups because of this. I shared this with Laura the night before and she seemed unconcerned. Sarah and her friends were not experienced hikers. They would not have moved at a fast pace and would likely have dawdled, caring more about the experience than the distance covered. Even in my slightly broken condition I would be faster than the distracted youths.

I met Laura downstairs at the reception of the hotel. As I suspected she was up, awake, and fully prepared. This was her way. The volunteer's cars were pulling up at the exterior of the hotel. We went out to the cars and, as predicted, Laura asked for her backpack. Damien handed her the backpack and in front of everyone she emptied it and began repacking it. Damien looked at me and I motioned to him to do nothing. He smiled at me and went back to concentrating on his own backpack. He moved the equipment around and handed me my backpack. I was going to be going in the car with the older officer, Laura sharing a ride with the younger.

We each got into our vehicles and headed towards the forest. As we wound up and around the bumpy roads it occurred to me that we would be passing the wreck of my car. I kept lookout for the wreck and was somewhat amused as we passed it. The carcass of the car did not look as bad as I had remembered. It was clear however that I would never be driving that vehicle again. I had expected a feeling of mourning as the car had served me well. With all the other emotions of the current situation I felt nothing. Perhaps a pang of guilt, not because I had crashed the car but because I did not care. As we arrived at the car park, I could see someone rummaging in the boot of Gus's car. I exited the car and shouted across at the man. He turned to look at me and I was surprised to see it was Gus standing there. In hindsight this should not have been a surprise. The man at the boot of the car was clearly a large individual. I had rarely seen anybody the size of Gus so it was unlikely that in the space of forty-eight hours I would have met two people of such volume.

Gus greeted us warmly but with a sombre tone in his voice. He had spent the last twenty-four hours looking for his friends but had found no sign of them. He was torn between concern and bemusement. His friends were experienced hikers who were able to take care of themselves, in most situations. Gus could not think of a situation that they could not handle. He saw the police officers behind me and moved to cover something in the trunk of his car. As I approached, he motioned to me to stay where I was and closed the trunk of his car. He came closer to me and asked me what we were doing. I got him up to speed with the situation, explaining that Sarah had still not appeared. I let him know that the men who were with me were going to help find her. We were to search three of the most popular paths in the forest looking for any sign we could of the group. Damien approached and introduced himself to Gus. Immediately there was a friendly competitiveness between the two. Any situation where you put two alpha males together will result in either friendly or non-friendly competition. Thankfully, in this situation, the competitiveness was nothing but friendly. Damien explained to Gus the three routes we were going to take. Looking them over Gus noted that one of those routes was not far from the route that he and his friends had planned to take. This was the route that Laura and the younger officer were to be taking. Gus offered and Laura accepted him to join that group. He felt that if his friends strayed from the path that was planned, this route would be the most likely location they would end up taking.

It was obvious that Gus was concerned for his friends. He had every right to be. What we had learned over the years indicates they met a horrific end. I remember thinking at the time that I would not want to be the person that upset Gus. He was a gentle giant, but he was a giant. And he was a very well-trained giant.

We each went our own way, agreeing to meet back in the car park in two days. No one would leave the car park until all three groups returned. In the event the one group did not return within six hours of the agreed time scale then one group would leave, and one group would stay. The group that left would go and get further help. The group that stayed would not venture from the car park. They would be the anchor by which any new activities would be bound. In our group of four I had the older police officer, whose name I learned was Henry. We had a farmer by the name of Edward who was headstrong, physically strong, and mentally strong. Rounding off the group was David, a slightly neurotic if highly intelligent young man. At the tender age of nineteen David had grown up with stories of the Redwood killer. He was fascinated by horror and violence. This was not abnormal for young men of that age. It was likely a phase he was going to grow out of. His eagerness for such macabre stories served us well in our search. He wholeheartedly embraced the Redwood legend. This meant if there was a bogeyman in the forest, we had one of the foremost experts on his history.

As we made our way into the forest it amazed me at how quickly the light was drowned by the height and thickness of the trees above us. Not pitch black but an eerie, shadowy darkness. Looking down you could barely see the forest floor beneath your feet. You could mostly make out what you were standing on but there was a lack of detail in what you saw. There was the occasional stumble as you stood on a branch which you thought would break but did not. The good news was you could usually identify the larger branches that cause a trip or serious fall. If you went over your ankle in this forest it was going to be a painful journey back to the car. Good time was made, especially considering the broken state of my body. We reached our first marker at the expected time of day. This was our first mini break, a chance to take on some fluids catch our breath and enjoy the clean, fresh air. We had walked through nothing but thick tree and bush and were two hours into our journey. Our expectation was to walk for between eight and ten hours before we reached our camping spot for the night. Once there we would get some rest, get back up at dawn and take a parallel route back. This allowed us to cover twice as much ground than normal hikers who would take the same route up and the same route back. Within the next hour of walking we would come to clearing with a river running through it.

We continued toward the clearing. We did not stop to enjoy the beauty of the area, and once past the clearing we were be back into thick forest of Redwood, pine, and other smaller species of tree. Ignoring the natural beauty of the area we saw nothing untoward. There was no sign of any recent tracks, no litter, no broken branches in unnatural places. No signs of any fires, camping equipment or personal belongings. It was eerily silent. You could hear yourself breathe. The only punctuations of sound were of animals in the thicket. We made it to our campsite without coming across a single being, or any sign of human interference to the natural area. Except for old unkempt fences from farms many years ago you would never have known the human beings existed on the planet.

Our campsite area was in a small clearing and we could see just up on the hill and to an old bothy. As the tents were being set up and fire lit, I decided I it would be prudent to check the building. If I were a curious youngster, that is the sort of activity I would undertake. I would want to get an impression of what life was like 100 years ago, when all you had was a one roomed house and an outside lavatory. Henry and Edward were not keen and tried to warn me away from investigating the area. It was not dark quite yet but to continue much further would have meant that we would have been camping in the middle of a forested area. We had gone as far, if not further, than we expected the youngsters could have got. But with still a few hours of daylight left I felt the pull to investigate the bothy on the hill. David was eager to join me and I did not want to dampen his enthusiasm. I did not see any danger in letting the youngster join me. Henry pulled David aside and told him not to go. David was not going to listen to Henry, David would not listen to me and David would not listen to Edward. David was going to do what David wanted to do.

We grabbed our torches just in case dusk came quicker than expected and we started to climb the field to the bothy. It did not take us long to get there and we started looking around the outside of the old building. There was nothing obviously untoward with the exterior, but there was an odd smell coming from inside the building. It was a rotting, musky smell that reminded me of what I experienced shortly after my car crash. Noticing my reaction to the smell, David became slightly more cautious. Walking toward an old building and looking at from the outside was a different proposition altogether from going inside the derelict shack. I told him he was more than welcome to stay outside. David had a stark choice either stay alone outside or face whatever was inside together. I was manipulating David, partially out of my own self-interest and partially because I did not like the idea of the poor boy standing outside on his own, afraid.

He bravely decided to join me in the bothy, and we pushed the door open. It was essentially a small room no more than five metres by three metres. You could see the old fireplace which had not been used for possibly a hundred years. It was dark inside; the roof was mostly intact, and the windows faced east so there was very little light coming into the building. We shone our torches inside to get visibility of what may be lurking in the shadows. As we moved our torches slowly around the walls and floor of the building, we could hear the buzzing of flies in the corner. Nothing prepared us for what we were about to see. As we reached the corner where both the smell and the noise were emanating from our torchlight entwined to reveal something which would haunt me for years to come.

In the corner of the building was the rotting corpse of a sheep. In and of itself this is a bearable, if slightly disgusting, sight. In this instance there was more than just the corpse; there was the mutilation. The sheep had been cut from gullet to anus. I am not an expert in decomposition but from the condition of the remains the sheep had been killed within the last seven days. Words cannot describe the viscera that was on display, nor can they truly convey the smell that emanated from that corner. Both David and I quickly exited the bothy. David turned left and I turned right, both of us holding the vomit in our mouth as we tried to direct the sick as far from ourselves as we could. I wiped my mouth with the napkin which was in my pocket and rummaged around for a second to give to David.

I handed David his napkin and he looked at me, tears in his eyes and his face white as a sheet. His hands were shaking, and you could see the fear in his soul. He did not say a word. He did not need to. We both felt the same uneasy feeling. His face told me that he thought this was the work of the Redwood killer. All I knew was it was the work of somebody who was severely disturbed.

We made our way down to the campsite and immediately Henry knew something was wrong. Explaining what we saw, Edward looked the most shocked of the group. Being a farmer, I am sure he could not imagine such brutality being carried out against livestock. His inclination was to go and look for himself to see if the horror was as bad as we described. We tried to convince him not to. You could see darkness was beginning to creep in. Edward insisted and started to make his way up the hill. Henry was clearly not going to venture that path with him and there was no way David was going to make a second trip. Although I was convinced whoever carried out this brutal act was far from the area, I did not want Edward going up their alone. I had an uneasy feeling about the group being split as it was, but a split of three and one was not acceptable. I followed Edward up to the bothy but refused to go back inside. I stood holding the door open as he shone his torch in the corner. Like David and I he shone around the room first before looking toward the main event. As Edward's eyes rested on the horror in the corner, he uttered just two words.

"The devil."

# CHAPTER 13

Dawn broke as the sun rose over the east and we each emerged from our tents shaken from the night before. The only one that seemed to manage to get a full night's sleep was Henry. He was also the only one that had not seen the mutilation. This was not coincidence. Henry did not even seem surprised at what we had found. We packed up our campsite and we took our planned route back to the car park. It was as uneventful was our trip out was. We saw no sign of humanity. My only hope was that one of the other groups had come across Sarah and her friends, or at least gained a clue of where they must have gone. As I was quickly learning hope was a fool's game.

All three groups arrived within a few hours of each other at the car park. As I knew Laura so well, I could tell by her face that they had found nothing either. Damien was harder to read but he quickly confirmed that they found no trace of Sarah or her missing friends. My heart sank further into my stomach. There was no positive way to look at this situation. How could a group of healthy young adults go missing without a trace? Laura and I took both police officers aside and asked them what the next step was. They confirmed to us that now was time to formally raise a missing person's report. I turned to Damien and inquired about other routes through the forest that may be more fruitful. He confirmed there were multiple other paths which we could take to continue the search. It became clear at this point that none of the other volunteers wanted to go back into the Forest. It seemed as we were talking to the officers Edward was sharing what we found in the bothy.

All but Damien refused to go back in the forest. It seemed whatever fear had prevented further volunteers from stepping forward had now gripped most of this group. I only had sympathy for David and Edward, who had seen the same horror I had. David was young and it was probably the first time he had encountered that side of humanity. However, mutilating a sheep and being violent towards another human being were two completely different things. While animal mutilation is often cited as a pathway to becoming a killer, there are many instances where it leads nowhere but to end the curiosity of the darker side of human behaviour.

My pleading with the group fell on deaf ears. Seven of the eight were going home and would not come out again. I had no doubts that once they reached the village the story of the mutilated sheep would spread. The vindictive side of me wanted to make a comment regarding the loss of the sheep cutting deeper than any other animal mutilation because of the local villages unnatural love for such creatures. This was below me and it was my anger it was driving me to think such things. I refrained from saying anything.

We let the others leave. That left just the four of us, as the police officers went back to the village with the residents. Considering the reaction of the other residents I was curious as to what Damien's motivations for staying were? I needed to be suspicious. Damien was curious about the legend, curious about the forest and curious missing people. In reality, my trip to the village, while for the most heart breaking of circumstances, led me to meeting two of the most upstanding people I had ever come across. We had searched the three main routes through the forest; however Damien had identified another five possible routes that could have been taken. Those five routes then branched out into another five routes each and so on, all the way through the forty-six square miles of forest. It was going to take years for just four of us to search such a large swath of land. We needed reinforcements.

We agreed to return to the village that evening, there was no value in continuing to search the forest at night. Once we got back to the hotel, we were politely informed that our rooms were booked from the following day onward and we would have to vacate. This was both a surprise and not. I could see Laura's ire rising and tried to calm her. We were going to be searching a forest, we did not need a hotel room. What we needed were warm bodies with a vested interest in a successful search. With sarcasm in every word I thanked the receptionist for her help. I made my way to my room, shut the door, and picked up the phone. It was time to involve the other families.

I phoned round each of the parents, none of whom were particularly worried when I started speaking to them. It seemed that their children were not as disciplined as Sarah when it came to communicating their where abouts. The group may have been young adults but in my mind young is the keyword. At that age there is still much bandwidth for mistakes and having a parent who cares and monitors and guides is still key during this phase of their child's life. By the time I had explained the situation to all sets of parents, they were rightfully worried. Had the vehicles not been in the car park I think each parent would have been calmer, expecting their child to have headed to the city to continue the good time. It was unlikely that they would extend such time in the forest without significant provisions. One or two nights in a forest with a group of friends be great fun, four nights would not be. At that point, the lack of hygiene facilities would begin to bite, especially for the younger women. I explained the hotel situation to the parents and the fact that we would need to go into the forest following several routes and camp. We wanted to involve the police, however the local officers were not going to be of much assistance. The time had come to go to the closest city and engaged the police there.

I met Gus and Laura in the pub for something to eat before we rested for the night. There was no room for Gus in the hotel, so Damien kindly agreed to put him up on his sofa. They seemed to be becoming fast friends. I explained the plan to head to the main city the next morning and meet the other families there, and to descend upon the police station and demand action. We ate the tasteless food and drank the bitter beer. This was not something I was going to miss. The rations we could carry while hiking would be Michelin star food compared the slop this local ale house served. We headed off to rest for the night, prepared to meet again in the morning and kick start the investigation into Sarah's disappearance.

The next morning we headed off early. We knew we would arrive at the city a couple of hours before the rest of the families. This would give us a chance to have something decent for breakfast and a proper cup of coffee. I had missed the conveniences of the urban setting. While villages are quaint, they are often backward and lacking in any real quality. The hostility of the village had meant I carried on uneasy anger toward them with me. Only Damien and David had been of any real assistance. We had agreed that we would meet Damien upon our return to the village. If needed he could cater for a couple of people however he did not have room for the numbers that were going to be joining us. In total we expected eight adults to be joining the four of us on our search through the forest. This was perhaps somewhat ambitious. It seemed a couple of the mothers did not want to join us in and wanted to work with the local police. They planned a campaign to uncover if any of their children have been seen anywhere locally in the last forty-eight hours.

We had our coffee and our breakfast at one of the local coffee shops in the city. Finally, a proper Cup of Java had passed my lips. Overall, this made me feel slightly better. As insignificant as it sounds, after several days of stress and anger and pain something close to home comfort can make a world of difference. We made our way to the police station and waited the short remaining time for the other families to arrive. Once there we wasted no time and headed into the police station to tell our story.

On entering the police station, we made our way straight to the sergeants' desk. I took the lead in explaining what was going on and he asked us to take a seat and wait while he relayed our story to somebody in the back. We did not have to wait long before a senior detective came to greet us. This immediately seemed strange to me. Is no one coming to take our statement or ask questions about our children? A senior detective would normally only be put onto a serious case where there was evidence of foul play. While I appreciate this would possibly accelerate our process, it did leave me curious as to why they bypassed basic protocol. The detective showed us through to the police briefing room, which was the only room large enough to hold all of us. It seemed that they did not want to speak to us individually, at least not to begin with.

The detective listened to the facts I laid out to him. He took scant notes, but I was reassured by the interested look in his eye. It was at this point I noticed the blinking red security camera in the corner of the room. To this day I still do not know if that room was permanently recorded or if the camera was switched on to capture our story. The detective excused himself and came back a short while later. He was flanked by another senior officer. They explained that they considered this as a missing person case and would be raised as such. Their next step would be to check with the local force and see that the paperwork was raised correctly. A couple of the fathers and myself protested loudly. We were asked to calm down and not raise our voices. The senior detective looked rather neutered, with the other officer taking the lead. I could only assume that this was chain of command. What I did not realise was this was not the first time the senior detective had been confronted by angry and distraught families.

We continued to push to no avail. The first step in the process was to get the missing persons profiles raised. More junior officers entered the room one by one they left with different members of the families to get descriptions of their children and what they were last known to be wearing. We were already fighting a losing battle against an establishment that did not want to help. The best we could do was follow the process until it failed. This was not going to stop me from investigating on my own and continuing the search of the forest. With continued pressure we got an agreement with the senior detective that he would join us the later in the day. This seemed to irk the more senior officer, whom we later found out was the lead detective for that area.

After the couple of hours, the officers had taken everybody's statements. We made our way back to the village as a group. Laura and I travelled with Gus and the rest of the parents followed. The detectives already knew the direction they were going in and said that they would meet us at the car park of the forest the following day. It was a quiet journey. We were in a car full of frustrated people feeling like the authorities had been of no support whatsoever. We were unable to bypass the village however we made a conscious decision not to stop and drive straight through to the forest road and onward to the car park. We could never have expected what we found. The two cars were gone. My initial reaction was to reach for my phone however there was no service in this area so even if Sarah and her friends had returned and taken the vehicles, I would not be able to call her.

Gus turned the car and we headed back down into the village. He parked outside the pub and looked at the cars in the area. We could not see the Range Rover nor the Fiat. I rushed into the pub, straight to the barmaid and asked her if she had seen Sarah or her friends. She looked at me puzzled. The barmaid was under the impression that they were still missing. I asked round the patrons of the bar if any of them had seen a group of youths passing through. I asked if they had seen the Range Rover or the Fiat. Nobody had seen anything.

I went back out to the car to tell Gus and Laura that Sarah and friends had not been seen. Gus drove us the short distance to the police stationed. Arriving at the same time with the detectives from the city I got out of the car and immediately shouted to the senior detective. I was keen to let him know what we had found, or not found in this case. His face was not one of surprise. He motioned for me to join him in the station. There we found Henry and the younger officer as relaxed as the day I had arrived. I relayed the news that the vehicles were gone from the car park. Henry implied this could be a positive turn of events. For him it meant that Sarah and her friends were okay and headed home. I checked my phone and saw that there was a reception, although a weak one. I tried Sarah's number but there was no luck. The call would not go through, her phone was either out of range or switched off.

Henry still seemed certain the group would be fine. He had begun the paperwork for the missing persons but said he no longer needed to complete it. If they had taken the cars and left the area it was no longer matter for the local police force. The senior detective who joined us from the city was more sceptical. There was no evidence that the group had returned to take their cars and no sightings of them driving through the village. That was certainly odd in a village where everybody watched every strangers move. The lead detective sided with Henry. He was happy enough to close the missing persons case and wait for the group to return home. I was aghast at this turn of events. I could not believe the Sarah and her friends, after being missing for three days, would just jump in their cars and drive home without calling any of their parents. Laura and Gus joined us in the police station. I could see that Laura's patience had gone beyond being worn thin and no longer existed. Gus was livid, towering over the lead detective grinding his teeth in anger. I did not envy the lead detective at this point, both my daughter and Gus directing their anger at him. He stood his ground although shakily. There were no missing persons in this area from his perspective. There was a group that spent longer in the forest than they had initially planned but had now left the area. Laura slammed her hands down on the nearest table.

"Unacceptable" she shouted.

The senior detective could see where this was going and there were only two possible outcomes. Laura and Gus in handcuffs or the police officers on the floor with bloodied faces. Neither was a particularly beneficial outcome, so I intervened with the support of the senior detective. The senior detective assured us that he would come up to the forest car park with us to examine the area for any signs of anything suspicious. The lead detective immediately shutdown the idea of any of the force heading up to the car park. Cleverly, the senior detective pulled aside his superior and muttered something under his breath to him. The lead detective looked at us, looked back to his subordinate and nodded. With that the senior detective guided us out. Laura took more persuasion than I and Gus took more persuasion then Laura but eventually we were convinced to leave the station.

Once outside the senior detective introduced himself more formally. His name was Xander; it transpired that he had grown up not far from this area. He knew of the history and the legend of the forest. He was not convinced that there was a monster that lurked in the darkness, however over the years he had seen too many missing persons cases swept under the carpet by the local authorities. He never understood why, however the outcome was always the result of pressure from above to close any case and write it off as another potential suicide. All missing persons cases in the area were written off as suicides after six months. It did not matter whether it was a group or an individual the outcome from the authorities was always the same.

We headed back up to the car park, families in tow. As we arrived Xander asked the Gus and me to help keep the other parents back as to not trample on any potential evidence. To placate my suspicions of him being involved in any coverup he allowed Laura to join him in his examinations. What they found created suspicion, if not evidence, of wrongdoing. Where the Range Rover had been parked there was broken glass. It looked as though somebody had smashed the driver side window of the car. There is no such evidence from where the Fiat sat, however that car had remained unlocked for four days. Laura, ever prepared, took photographs of what they had found. Xander seemed disappointed and I was curious as to why. Why would a detective be disappointed that there was some sort of evidence? He explained to me that this just deepened his suspicions that something was very wrong in the area. That in itself did not disappoint him, but he knew this was going to be another case which was put into a dark box and written off as suicide in six months.

With no other options in front of us and the prospect of no help from the authorities I rallied the other parents as best I could. Gus drove to the village to collect Damien and the two of them arrived back in a caravan of cars. Damien covered the area on a map with the other parents and we decided to split into four groups. I would lead one group. Gus would lead another of the groups, as would Laura. Damien would lead the final group. We tried to keep families together as best we could. We knew we had a lot of ground to cover and everybody had a vested interest in finding the youngsters. Time was running out, if something bad had happened, if our children needed help, it would soon be too late. Xander would not join us on the search. the lead detective would not allow it. He would return to the village, report what he had found and wait for the officers to officially bury the story.

Damien identified four campsites on four different routes which we would be able to reach within two to three hours of trekking. It was getting later in the day, so we did not want to be walking too far into the forest when night fell. We had three days to search the forest and return to our vehicles. Anything beyond that, with this group, would have become a challenge. Most parents where urbanites. They had never trekked through a forest let alone camped. We had limited equipment and no way with which to communicate with the other groups. We had to be concise in our planning and limited in our time scales. If we did not find our children during the search, we did not know what the next steps would be.

What transpired was seventy-two hours a fruitless trekking through a dark, empty, and lonely forest. There was no evidence of human activity found on any of the four routes we took. The small mercy was that we found no evidence of animal mutilation on these four paths either. We returned to the car park after three days exhausted, emotionally defeated, and uncertain of what the future held.

# CHAPTER 14

As with many local legends, the stories of the Redwood massacre and the Redwood killer have various strands. With the core of the story being the same, the farmer who murdered his family, divergence begins with what happens in the following forty years. One such theory is of copycats. This is the only plausible non-supernatural explanation for forty years of missing people. This explanation itself is deeply flawed and for those with an open mind is less believable than some of the more fantastical theories.

With so many missing people the reality is suicide is nothing but a cover up story designed by the authorities to keep people as far from the reality of what happened to the relatives and loved ones. The theory of copycats piggybacks on stories of copycats of other serial killers and mass murderers. It automatically assumes that over forty years there has been a steady turnover of copycat killers working in the same area of the country.

For this to be feasible each killer must hand the

torch to a new psychopath or there is a cult which cultivates killers from young age and swaps them out at regular and necessary intervals. When you delve into the reality of the missing persons cases you realise the sheer impossibility of copycat or multiple killers. To support this, you would need to make a number of assumptions which viewed alone are believable, however stacked together create almost an impossible possibility.

Each killer would need to be brought into the world with the same mental deficiencies or lack of emotion as the previous killer. Contrary to popular belief sociopaths are rare. It is even rarer for a sociopath to kill. You are more likely to come across a sociopath running a billion-dollar company than you are killing another human being. The personality traits of a sociopath are far more aligned to what is required to be successful in high pressure business than to kill.

To kill on the scale of the Redwood killer you would need to be emotionless about your acts of violence. Only a sociopath lacks empathy with their victims. Other killers, who could be classed as psychopaths, usually carry anger or guilt and a feeling of sexual inadequacy. If the Redwood killer were your garden variety psychopath there would be large amounts of evidence strewn throughout the forest. The controlled and precise nature of criminality and brutality in the forest to leave no trace evidence indicates a highly sophisticated killer. To find a sociopath in this area would be one in a million. To find the succession of sociopaths in this area for a period of forty years would be astronomically improbable.

Any killer in a forest such as the Redwood would have to have unparalleled local knowledge. They would need to be able to avoid detection and to be able to surprise groups of young fit individuals. They would also require the strength and agility to kill them. The organisation required to cultivate killers and impart the knowledge of the area would be military in scale. To be able to blend with your environment, to be able to kill almost unseen and unheard is not the modus operandi of a normal person. Serial killers tend to be good at blending into the local environment. This would indicate that the killer would be somebody in the village. However, over a forty-year time span one would imagine the village would tire of a killer on their doorstep. If this killer were amongst the villagers, he would almost certainly have been dealt with by either the authorities or a local mob. Again, this would point to some sort of cult or other satanic organisation. This would leave evidence and an organisation of this size would require a base of operations which would be nigh on impossible to hide. Although the forest is large it would be easy to spot any land which was being used for such nefarious purposes. The forest is surrounded on all sides by areas that would make such an establishment impossible. To the South you have the village and to the north you have inhospitable mountains. To the west travelling through the village you reach dead end marked by a scrap yard. The scrap yard is a mountain of broken cars and metal. The only building an old shack made from corrugated steel. Inside a desk, lamp and a gentle man who kindly offers to crush your car every time you visit. East of the forest is an old military communications bunker from World War Two. Still owned by the military, it is guarded by two full time stationed military officers. Over the years the military base has seen several attempts of scavengers trying to liberate World War Two memorabilia from its rooms. As such the military has a regular rotation of guards. It is often discussed as to what to do with this bunker in the future years. The military continues absorbing the cost of maintaining a bunker the many private collectors would love to bring into their ownership.

The expertise in which evidence is cleared once more points to a single efficient, effective killer. Multiple killers would surely develop their own signatures. Add to this serial killer's penchant for trophies and attention. Very few serial killers do not enjoy the spotlight and the chase of the authorities. To stay one step ahead of well-funded law enforcement agencies gives a serial killer an immense feeling of power and control. It is unlikely that multiple killers over a long period of time would shun this trend.

The Redwood killer is almost certainly a lone individual carrying out unspeakable acts of evil. The concept of one copycat is ludicrous. I would be willing to bet my life but there is not, nor will there ever be, copycats of the Redwood killer.

# CHAPTER 15

With our own search proving fruitless we had no option but to return to the authorities. After three days almost all the families had to return home to deal with the realities of life as was now in front of them. The two who stayed behind to try and coordinate with the police had found nothing but obstruction from the authorities. The only responsive officer was Xander, the senior detective who seemed frustrated at the inaction over the years of the local and regional police forces. We did not know what to do next. Our children were missing, and authorities were not interested. We were not in a position where we wanted to declare them dead, it was far too early for that. We knew that with the time that had passed it was the most likely scenario. There had been no contact from any of the children for over a week. Nobody had seen them since the day they left the village for the forest. What do you do when you have a hole in your life and no closure? Who do you turn to? How do you move on?

For me there was no moving on. I kept pressuring the authorities as long as it was possible, eventually the police stopped returning my calls. I contacted local newspapers who had no interest in carrying my story. National papers would not touch my tale, it was too fantastical. There was no evidence that anything had happened other than youths who had run away from home. I managed to convince one dark rag to carry the story. It usually ran stories about celebrity relationships or mutated bats carrying deadly diseases in their fangs. It was not a newsworthy publication, but it was the only publication that would carry any story about Sarah and her friends. The issue that was released could be best described as absolute trash. Squeezed on the pages of the glossy publication were stories of haunted mansions and government super soldier experiments.

The story written of Sarah and her friends did not focus on them going missing nor did it focus on a village full of empty souls. It focused on the history of the parents and theorised about what home environment would want to make children runaway and never contact anybody. They questioned whether they were part of a satanic cult that had gone to the forest for group suicide, ignoring the fact that this would leave evidence and bodies. It created a fictional story out of a real-life tragedy, one that was even more absurd than that of the Redwood killer. Every note of fact and comment given was twisted. All the publication cared about was selling issues.

For many of the families this was the last straw. My campaign to find the truth lost the support of those who should have been most committed to its success. One by one the families fell, each looking for their own form of closure. They began to accept the group suicide theory put forward by the police. They stopped questioning why there was no evidence. They stopped asking where the camping equipment was and where were the bodies. I wish I could be angry with them for abandoning me when I needed them. I understand their decision though, the pain of facing reality far outweighs the disappointment of accepting a lie. I was alone. Laura was beginning to feel the strain of the search and did not enjoy the media attention I was trying to bring to the family. She was always a private person and did not want people looking into her history, bringing up her mistakes. She never accepted the official line from the authorities of suicide, but she also did not believe the stories of a Redwood killer. Gus stood by my side as best he could, a constant companion for a long time. However even he had to return to an element of normality; to try and continue his life. He carried a burden of guilt that crushed him despite his giant frame. He had to explain to his friend's parents what had happened and why he was not there to protect them. To their credit none of them blamed Gus. These were experienced, mature and well-trained adults. If they could not look after themselves in this situation with the skills they had acquired over the years, Gus's presence would have been unlikely to change what happened. For Gus that was never enough.

Damien had been hounded out of the village. The price for him helping us was his home, his way of life. He did not move far but he became a pariah. He lived a few miles outside the village in an old gate house surrounded by nothing but trees, pheasants, deer, and the occasional noise of birds of prey flying overhead. He was still fascinated by the forest and was keen to continue his research and investigation. He just had to do it from slightly further out.

Young David, who had witnessed the same horror I had in the bothy on the hill, had moved to the city. He was found to be the webmaster for the Redwood massacre website I had visited. He continued to run the website, continued his fascination with the legend, however it was done from afar and in between a life that now included full time work and a dog named Faith.

Xander, the senior detective, had tried to help us as best he could, and it almost cost him his career. The damage it had done to his reputation within the force simply for trying to help terrified families had also put a strain on his marriage. He had been given all the worst investigations that the police could throw his way and he swallowed them like the shit sandwiches they were. It was the only way to get back in the good graces of the force. It did not matter the reality was he would likely never to be fully accepted back in. He had to try. Over time he repaired his marriage and partially repaired his reputation in the police force. Fate has a funny way of changing your life. Just as life began to balance for Xander his wife became ill. It was not an illness from which she was going to recover nor was it an illness that was going to give her much time left on the earth. Xander the only officer who cared what happened to my daughter was about to lose the only person he had ever loved.

I continued my research into the Redwood legend. I developed a research relationship with David, who was keen to keep looking into his local area history. Through our research we found sixty-nine confirmed missing cases and anecdotal evidence of a further one hundred and sixty-two possible missing people. There was extraordinarily little evidence of supernatural or violent activity prior to 1972. With the exception of the Celtic legend of the forest bodach, all seemed normal about this eerie death trap. We made one small breakthrough finding the name of one of the junior police officers who investigated the original 1972 case. To my surprise it, turned out to be the elderly gentleman I had conversed with my first morning outside the police station.

I was keen to find out more about what happened that summer in 1972. I was not welcome back in the village, and David had fewer connections then when he lived there. He had one friend willing to help us contact the retired police officer. That initial contact did not go well. The officer did not want to speak about the summer of 1972, of what he had seen. Nor did he want to speculate what had happened since.

For our research to be more successful and for me to be able to bring the group back together to continue the search for Sarah and her friends an event of significant magnitude would have to occur.

# CHAPTER 16

Three years had passed since Sarah and her friends had gone missing. My investigation had gone cold and the group who helped us search when Sarah went missing had disbanded. Although I kept in touch with most of them, we were scattered across the country. Laura had tried to get back to some semblance of normality but was struggling, as was I.

Late in the summer of 2013 after three dormant years there was a chilling story coming out of the Redwood forest. It was David who first contacted me to let me know of another group of youths who had gone missing in the forest. Five had entered and only one had come home. Her story was that of horrific violence, pain, and torture. For the first time in forty years there was a survivor. Her name was Pamela.

Pamela's story has become well documented over the years, even being turned into a movie and a bestselling novel. While both tell a compelling story, they play fast and loose with the actual police report that Pamela filed. When I heard that a survivor had been found alive and physically, if not mentally, unharmed I knew that this was the jump start my investigation needed. Surely with a survivor the authorities would have to take a more serious interest in the Redwood forest.

Again, I was proven to be wrong. The police's initial suspicion fell on Pamela, as if this five-foot five-inch, one hundred and five pound girl would be able to easily slaughter four of her friends. Had she even been in a position to do so, she would have been unable to dispose of the bodies and the equipment. There was no time to destroy the evidence which would have been scattered across the forest. When Pamela was found she was near the old junkyard. Soaked in blood, terrified and barely able to string a sentence together, it took a couple of days in hospital before she was able to pull together a coherent story of what happened. During that time forensic tests were run over her clothes. The police report claimed that, while they could confirm none of the blood was Pamela's, there was too much cross contamination to get any matches. Any samples which were of sufficient quality to get a single individuals DNA from were lost as part of the chain of custody between the police and the laboratory. Shortly after the tests were run the laboratory had a fire. In its twenty-three year history there had never been a single accident at the site. Upon the appearance of trace evidence of a Redwood killer there was a mysterious fire. Investigations could not pinpoint where or how the fire started however it was put down as a tragic accident. What made the accident tragic was the death of the laboratory assistant, who had reached out to Xander about previous cases and what had been found in the evidence collected from Pamela.

While Xander, now a widower, was no longer part of the police force he still had a handful of friends who fed him information on the case. He shared with me the story that Pamela had relayed to the police.

Pamela and her friends entered the forest and within twenty-four hours Pamela was the only one left standing. A large, masked killer picked off her friends in the forest. As she made her way for help, she came across an old, abandoned farm. There were no signs of life in the house, yet the vast outbuildings had an unsettling echoing noise coming from within. Desperate for help she went inside, where she came across the Redwood killer. She described him as standing at near seven feet tall. While likely to be an embellishment, her fear would have played tricks on her senses so to her he may have seemed such a size. She described him as a hulking man, wearing dungarees and a flannel shirt. His mask was made from a burlap sack and had indentations where the eyeholes should be. She never saw an ounce of humanity in his actions and never saw the face under the mask. The buildings seemed like a labyrinth to her and their described size narrowed the location where these events could have occurred. While in this prison like environment Pamela witnessed her friends being mutilated and murdered. Although uncertain if any were still alive, she feared for her life and fled. As she tried to make her way out the farm, she came across a man she described as both comforting and terrifying. He too was searching for his daughter and narrowed the possibilities of her killer's location to this farm. She never learned the man's name, but he was described as around six feet tall with a local accent and a big shotgun. He never made it out. Pamela described how he took a stand against Redwood killer as she ran. She heard his screams echoing through the building as she made her way towards what she hoped was an exit.

Pamela managed to escape the farm but had no idea where she was. Luckily, after an unknown amount of running, she came across a road, better described as an old farm track. On it drove a car which stopped to help her. As the man exited the vehicle Pamela, terrified, cold, and tired, did not know whether to trust him or run. Before she could decide the Redwood killer appeared behind him and took his life in the most horrific manner. Pamela ran once again and before long she was in the old junkyard. Realising she did not know where she was, did not know the local terrain and was weak and exhausted with fear she faced the reality that she might not escape this alive. It was at this point Pamela noticed the crane in the middle of the junkyard, which had been left with a car hanging from his claw thirty feet above the ground. There was only one way she could see to get into the cab of the crane and that was by going under the car. She ran as fast as her legs would take her and climbed into the cab. She had no idea what she was doing, thinking she was looking for a big red button with words 'release' on it. There was none. She managed to start the machine up. In a remote area such as this there was no reason for the owner of the crane to remove the keys from the cab. There was not supposed to be anybody for miles. The crane lit up the junkyard and Pamela saw the Redwood killer, still and staring in her direction. He started his stalk and made his way in her direction as she desperately tried to find the button to release the car from the cranes grip. There were too many buttons and not enough information to find what she was looking for.

In frustration and fear she slammed her hands down. The crane lurched, the claw sprang open and with a bang released the car. The broken vehicle fell thirty feet to the ground, creating a huge plume of dust and dirt. Pamela peered out of the cab of the crane, waiting for the cloud to settle. She refused to move until she had full sight of what happened. If the Redwood killer was still alive, she just was not going to make her death easy for him. He was going to have to come to her. A few moments passed, described as an eternity of hell, before Pamela could see only the car where the standing monster had been. Slowly she exited the cab and made her way down to where the car sat. She looked left, right, up, down, and back to make sure there were no surprises. As she reached the car, she could see an arm under it, twitching. The movement stopped. Coating the arm was the flannel shirt of the Redwood killer. Pamela described how she fell to her knees, tears running down her face. She's since said she wished she could come up with some witty one liner like they did in the movies, but the reality was the only noise she made was sobbing. The car had landed perfectly on top of the monster and was sitting flat, wheels down on the ground.

Pamela walked from the junkyard in the only direction she could, walking as far as the single road would take her. She did not reach the village but met an old man walking his dog. Fate would have it that this was the police officer who was part of the original 1972 investigation. The same man who refused to help me in my investigation. Coming across another victim of the Redwood killer triggered the deep guilt this man felt for his inaction over the previous forty years. It was only a few days after this said he sent me the notes from the original investigation and within two weeks he had peacefully passed away in his home with his dog by his side.

At first Pamela was treated as a suspect in the murder of her friends. The man she described who helped her in the farm was found to be Edward, the farmer who was part of our initial search. His daughter had gone missing in the Redwood forest with some friends in the intervening years, one of the anecdotal and unreported events. It seemed that anyone from the village who went missing from the village was not reported to the police. The locals knew what had happened to them, there was no point and investigating or searching. That would likely only lead to the deaths of others.

The driver who stopped to help Pamela was the owner of the junkyard. He had worked beside the forest for almost thirty years without incident. It was later discovered he was pivotal in the cover up the village was perpetrating.

There is no evidence that the police could use to tie Pamela to the murder of her missing friends. Again, they put it down to suicide and cast Pamela as the traumatised and distraught survivor of a suicide pact. Psychiatrists at the local hospital put her story down to survivors' guilt. They claimed she had manufactured a fantastical story based off a local urban legend. Arrogant that their cover up would be accepted as normal, the police never tried to explain the vast quantities of human blood which covered Pamela when she was found. She was placed under the psychiatric care of the local authorities until such time as she was just deemed not to be a danger to herself or others.

This was the break I needed. Media interest in Pamela Story was high, however again they distorted the facts to paint her as either a lunatic or a killer. The village was inundated with reporters they tried to keep a united front. There were stories of mob anger towards journalist's and violence caught on camera as the locals forced the outsiders from the local establishments.

I tried reaching out to speak to Pamela. Being under lock and key I could not get access to speak to her. Ashamedly I resorted to underhanded tactics. I contacted the head psychiatrist at the hospital she was being held in and claimed to be another grieving survivor of the Redwood forest. I could help in Pamela's treatment. I explained to the doctor that I too had had auditory and visual hallucinations as well in the Redwood forest and it took me time to accept the reality that there was no Redwood killer. I spoke of the help others had given me who had been in a similar situation. I told them it was key to my recovery. None of this was true by now I was convinced of the Redwood killer legend and all I wanted was to know where Pamela had been attacked.

# CHAPTER 17

Pamela's survival and story were the fresh impetus I needed to restart my search, this time with support. The death of her friends and her subsequent discovery were a blessing. I could use this as a fulcrum round which to assemble a squad to hunt the Redwood killer once more. I reached out to various contacts and friends, looking to build a team who could find this monster and help me kill him.

First on my list was Laura. An obvious choice, she had suffered almost as much as I from her sister's disappearance. Laura was more than happy to join, despite our strained relationship. Laura had been a difficult child as well. She was almost the opposite of Sarah. Where Sarah was respectful, polite, and popular, Laura was more distant and constantly found herself disagreeing with my rules and dreams for her. She never got into any serious trouble when she was a youngster, but she was never what you would call a young lady. Her fiery temper often got her into confrontations from which she refused to back down. Her need for excitement and danger led her to racing cars, skydiving, mountain climbing and a variety of other "sports" where it would be easy to lose your life. When she joined the army, it was a relief. It is strange to think that as a father you would feel your daughter was safer in a conflict zone then at home. It was in the army that Laura learned to channel her anger and her need for danger. She also learned responsibility for others, a lesson I had not managed to teach her during her formative years. When she left the army, she was still headstrong and could still have a fiery temper, but she was disciplined. Laura never shared what she saw in her army days, nor what her missions were. She was, and remains to this day, very secretive about it. She came out of the army with an empathy I had not seen in her before but that was not to be mistaken for weakness. She was an expert in hand to hand combat, trained to use multiple weapons and was, by all accounts, a walking weapon. Her time now was spent helping vulnerable woman build their confidence, strength, and self defence. She ran an outreach program helping those who were struggling in abusive relationships, or that had recently left such a coupling. She still worked with the military sometimes as a special advisor, although I was never aware what branch. There is a strength she now has that I could never attain, and I continue to try and help her succeed in life. She had turned into a formidable woman, and although we still had our differences, she would be key in leading the team.

Gus was more than happy to join us, however I could sense his scepticism. His brotherly bond with Laura meant that he would be there whenever she needed and whenever she asked. Gus is a jovial giant. He brought a light-hearted warm quality to the group. Immediately Laura and he bonded. As I got to know Gus more it became clear why. Gus had been military as well and was part of a well-respected special forces unit. When we first met, he was going hiking with his friends, both of whom had military backgrounds. They met in an unnamed warzone they officially were not meant to be. He had saved both their lives on countless occasions and they his. This is one of the reasons their disappearance was so confusing. Two well trained former military men vanishing without a trace in a forest which should have posed them no challenge. The other side of that coin is the being former military men it made the police's job writing it off as suicide easier. Post-traumatic stress disorder they claimed. Such a statement by the police was disrespectful to their memory and disrespectful to Gus. As a team they had faced numerous enemies in hostile conditions and lived to tell the tale. One had suffered upon their return, his mental trauma being a constant reminder of the horrors of war. With the help of Gus, others in the squad and counselling he had moved into a more stable part of his life. Gus told me what you see in war never leaves you, and neither do the things you do. Even if they are part of the greater good, he told me, taking another's life is a stain on your soul. Like Laura, Gus did not speak much about his time in the military. I endeavoured to find out more about him, this gem of a man who had entered my life by saving my life. I reached out to various former squad members with whom he served. Most were reluctant to speak, except for sharing how much they owed him and how much they admired him. One story that was shared demonstrated the kind of man Gus is. The unit were serving in an unnamed desert area, which I assume was either Iraq or Afghanistan, going door to door in a mostly abandoned town looking for any families who had yet to leave. There they came across a woman in hysterics, refusing to leave her home. Through their translator the squad came to learn her husband had been killed by local insurgents and her eight year old boy was missing. She would not leave without him. Gus commanded his troops to stay with the mother while he and one other went to search for the boy. Gus's companion for this was one of the men he was meant to go hiking with. Gus searched house to house for the boy, aware that any door may have an improvised explosive device attached. They found him around half a mile from his home. The boy was tired and hungry, but otherwise unharmed. They took the boy and rapidly made their way back. As they rounded a corner, they encountered enemy combatants who immediately opened fire on them. Taking cover on either side of the street, they returned fire but were outnumbered. Gus's squad mate noted the building next to him could be used as a route away from the enemy, heading toward the mothers' home. As suppressing fire was laid down, Gus scooped the boy up and ran across the street and bursting through the door to the building. His squad mate joined him, and they made a hasty exit through the back. As they exited they threw a grenade into the building to slow anyone following them. They managed to get away, and as the slowed it became apparent that Gus had not gotten away unscathed. He had taken two bullets, one to his upper left arm and one through his upper left trapezius muscle. He continued carrying the boy in his right arm while his companion provided ongoing cover at the rear. They managed to get back to the mother and reunite what was left of the family. Although his injuries were serious, they were not life threatening. Gus returned to active duty after a short rehabilitation. Due to the nature of their mission, he did not receive any official commendation for his brave actions. When I asked him about this Gus informed me the only commendation he ever needed was the ongoing letters he received from the boy. A common perception is that the military breeds killers however in my experience I have seen more compassion and empathy from most former military operatives than I see from the average man or woman on the street.

I strongly felt we needed a local expert on the team, so I reached out to Damien. As a true student of the local area he would know where buildings of such size as Pamela described were in the forest confines. It was likely a lot of these derelict buildings would not show up on any maps, and the proximity of the old military base meant not satellite imagery was available. We could also use the rough time scale we had received from the police notes between Pamela leaving the farm and coming across the junkyard. With someone like Damien on the team we could develop an extremely focused plan on finding this monster. Damien was keen to explore more of the forest, and that was his main driver. He still did not believe in the Redwood killer, but he was intrigued by the idea that such a beautiful area had become suicide central for so many people. It was a dichotomy he could not ignore. Damien also brought a laid-back approach, which I felt could help relax the team. There was no doubt trying days ahead of us and as much as I believe structure is important you do need someone who works from their gut. Damien was very much that person. During our early engagements he would often plan then within a few hours completely change his approach based on what he found or felt. His flexibility helped us constantly re-evaluate what we were doing, keeping us assured we were following the best process.

Damien was a physically fit man, strong and agile. He had a certain confidence one has when you know you are attractive. That translated into an easy going charm the made him instantly likeable. He was scruffy round the edges, not one for designer clothes or equipment. This seemed to give him an added quality, the ruggedness attractive to most. He had spent enough time trekking and camping to be quite a skilled outdoorsman, and I had no doubt if things got rough, he could handle himself.

We reached out to David, who was reticent to get involved at first. He would not join us in the forest. His previous experiences had scared him. He was young and meek, and in all truthfulness was not built for what we were likely to face. His knowledge of the Redwood legend was what we needed from him, and for that he did not need enter the forest. He would act as our central support team. His analytical mind would help us collate information. With that we could attempt to use empirical and non-empirical data to better define our ongoing activities. David excelled at this type of activity, and his computer skills were better than most. His time in the forest had left him even more fearful of what may lay in the woods. He was an anxious person at the best of times, and he was now more withdrawn than he ever had been. I was concerned that even knowledge of what we find would be damaging to his fragile psyche however his computer skills and knowledge of the legend were too important to not have.

Xander was relatively easy to convince to come back. With his wife and his career gone he had nothing left to lose. Xander had a great investigative mind. As such he was not driven by gut or instinct but by analysis and logic. Almost like a modern day Sherlock Holmes, Xander's powers of observation and deduction were a sight to behold. Despite the way the police treated him he was still loyal to them in many ways. He believed that, although our experience had told us otherwise, if we could gather some concrete evidence the authorities would do the right thing. I knew that he would find clues none of the rest of us could. We were investigating a crime, and having an experienced detective on our side, even a retired one, was going to be of huge benefit. He would also help us avoid making any mistake with any evidence we found. His knowledge of police and forensic process meant that we would not make the same simple mistakes other private investigators do. He would help keep us on the right side of the science. During our communications Xander let me know that recently two others had been in contact with him, having seen his name in the papers around the time of Sarah's disappearance.

Jennifer was a psychological profiler who was fascinated with the type of mind that could commit such atrocities. While she did not necessarily believe in the Redwood killer, she was interested in studying not only such a monstrous person but also those who would hunt search a dangerous prey. As part of her deal to come along we all had to agree to be profiled by her. She wanted to make sure there were no loose cannons on the trip and was hoping to release a study on killers and the victim impact. While slightly insulted, thinking myself beyond such profiling, I did realise the benefits of ensuring the team were mentally stable before venturing into the forest and facing whatever demons lay therein. Jennifer had worked with the authorities profiling several sadistic cases. She had assisted in both serial killer and mass killer crimes. Her success rate in profiling was, according to Xander, one of the highest ever seen. At one point she postulated on a killer's hair colour based on several characteristics found at the crime scenes, and was proven to be accurate almost to the shade. She could read people within minutes based purely on their language, body positioning, tone of voice and facial expressions. She would constantly prove doubters wrong by inviting them to a game of poker. She never lost. As much money as she made from profiling, she made twice as much from poker. Jennifer proved to be confident and fearless, and identified almost immediately where we would likely have personality clashes in the team. This allowed us to carefully manage how we worked as a squad, ensuring everyone was happy and that we were using everyone's skills as effectively as possible.

Our final group member was Liam. Liam's parents had gone missing twenty years earlier when he was just a young boy. They had come to the village on the Redwood forest for a romantic getaway. They were not experienced hikers or campers and had only driven to the forest for short walk. All they wanted was to see the natural beauty of the trees and the rivers surrounded by heather. Like so many others they never returned from their forest trip. Although not obsessed with the Redwood legend when he heard of Pamela's survival and subsequent story it brought up repressed feelings of guilt and anger. He had been a difficult child and in his mind, in his guilty conscience, his parents would have not taken the weekend away had he not been such a spoiled child. Liam was full of confidence and bravado but was also impetuous and brash. His manner and approach could rub people up the wrong way, but they quickly realised his intentions and youthfulness, and he was forgiven. Jennifer let me know his attitude stemmed from insecurity. He was the youngest and least experienced of the group, except David whom no you man would see as a threat. As such Liam was overcompensating which led to his sometimes infuriating approach. Within a short space of time Liam found his place in the team. This settled the teething problems he had joining the group, and he quickly made friends with all the team. His relationship with David became particularly strong, and he often acted as protector when the humour became a bit rough.

With such a mix of personalities and backgrounds it was good to have two leaders such as Laura and Gus.

We had our search party, now all we needed was a plan. We were not welcome in the village, so we were going to have to set a base of operations a couple of hours away. This was not going to be a straight-forward two day search. We were all committed to spending the next eight weeks investigating the forest and the facts around Pamela's reappearance. We rented a cottage not far from where Damien lived and descended like a militia from hell.

# CHAPTER 18

Damien had divided forest into eight sections. He had identified the most likely group of buildings that Pamela was describing, based on the location of the junkyard and the time she thought she spent running from the Redwood killer. The police had refused to search the buildings due to the fact there was no evidence of the Redwood killer. No body was found in the junkyard when they got there, two days after Pamela's reappearance. They put the delay in searching the junkyard down to the incoherent nature of Pamela's story. In reality it was either unwillingness or incompetence. If I were a gambling man, I would put my money on a combination of the two. There was something larger which was holding the police back from fully investigating what was going on in the Redwood forest.

This time we were going to go in as one team. Based on what happened to Pamela we were not going to take any chances. When Gus arrived, he opened his trunk and showed us his friends, who he had taken along for the ride. Ma and Pa, as he called them, were an Uzi and a Glock. Under them he uncovered big Bubba, an old World War Two heavy machine gun. That, we assured him, we would not need. He also had a shotgun and another two handguns. There is no question about the legality of these weapons however considering our current situation we all decided it was better to have than to have not. Laura and Xander were the only two of the group with any formal firearm training but we were in a remote enough area that we could pass any shooting practice off as hunters nearby. As Damien, Laura and I planned our activities over the coming eight weeks, Gus taught the others the basics of shooting. David was the only one who declined. He was not going to join us in the forest but collate the information we brought back from our base in the cottage. As such he felt he had no need for such training and was not a keen fan of firearms anyway. Firing a handgun is not that difficult. The target is close enough there is a good chance you are going to hit it. Gus was an excellent shot, so we were relying on him for any targets that were more than ten feet from us. Laura was a sharpshooter. In her army days she had undergone various training camps and she excelled in shooting. As such Gus would carry the Uzi and Laura would carry a handgun. I would take a handgun as would Jennifer. Xander would take the shotgun. Damien was more than happy just to have his fists on his feet. Liam wanted a weapon however in all honesty he was more of a liability then an asset while armed. We feared if he were to carry a gun any enemy we came across would be safer than the rest of us would be.

Our plan was to start our search at the junkyard and move through the forest to the nearest large farm. With the owner of the junkyard being dead and no nearby known relatives the junkyard was chained up. Breaking those chains would not be difficult and it was remote enough that we should not arouse suspicion. The police claimed they had searched the junkyard thoroughly but based on our experiences with them it was more than likely they barely looked in the front gate. Should the search not be successful there was another large farm a few miles further into the forest. That would be our second outing. We planned each outing to last no more than three days, with rest in between at the cottage. It was mentally exhausting with all we had gone through, and all that was riding on our success. Depending on what we found we did not know what time we would need to recover either our bodies or our mind. We planned approximately two searches a week for the next eight weeks to try and cover as much of the forty-six square miles as we could. We did not tell anybody in the village what was happening, and we did not alert the authorities that we would be there. To do so would create trouble that we were not going to back down from. We may have been a small group, but we had a purpose and a cause. Nobody was going to stop us from finding the truth.

# CHAPTER 19

The day we arrived at the junkyard was overcast and cold. Summer was coming to an end and in this part of the country that meant wind and a chill from the north. We split into groups of two to search the junkyard. The footprint of the industrial area was not large however the broken-up cars and trailers were stacked high. One would have to question the health and safety implications of stacking metal so high. The central area where Pamela's story had the car falling on the Redwood killer was clear. There was an indentation where she claimed the car would have fallen but no sign of any blood or a body. We were curious as to where the car she claimed she had dropped could be. Although like something out of an action movie, we did not doubt the story she had told. Laura and I stood centrally, looking around are the stacked-up cars when we saw a small four door car sitting perked against the sight of one of the towers of metal. As we examined the area closer you could see faint evidence that the car had been moved recently, with some faint drag marks near where it was placed. It was on its side parked against a stack of crushed vehicles. We looked around the vehicle, it matched the description of what Pamela had given but again there is no obvious evidence over anything untoward other than recent movement. What we really needed to see was the underneath the car; this is where having a brute such as Gus comes in particularly handy.

Gus joined us and we wrapped a chain around the supporting bars on the car door. Damien, Liam and Xander offered to help but Gus waved them away big smile adorning his happy face. This was the sort of thing Gus lived for. With one big heave he pulled, and the car rocked. It looked as though it was going to roll but then settled back into position. Gus mumbled something under his breath, and you could see him gritting his teeth. He was not going to be beaten by this car. And he was not going to accept anybodys help. With a deep breath he pulled again. This time the car did not rock, it rolled towards Gus. As it looked like it was going to lurch and do another 360 degrees it fell back down onto its roof, wheels in the air. Gus laughed and slapped his shoulders before wandering over to join us to looking at the bottom of the car. Weeks had passed since Pamela's reappearance and the weather been unpredictable, with heavy rain and sunshine combining with strong winds. This was going to have an impact on any physical evidence we would find. The bottom of the car looked mostly like the bottom of a car should. There were a few out of place dents on some of the underside engine components but nothing that would make you overly suspicious. As we followed along the exhaust pipe there was a strange brown patch of colour. To me it was obvious that this was blood. Gus and Laura were both sceptical. This could be blood but there is no way of proving it with the equipment we had. If a car was dropped on a human being, we would expect to see more mess. Xander was the only trained detective amongst us and he spent considerable time looking around the car and examining the bottom. We continued to search the junkyard without success as Xander went over the car with a fine-tooth comb. We spent several hours at the junkyard and needed to move on if we were going to be able to camp in the forest before darkness fell. We reconvened with Xander and he updated us on it what he had found.

Xander managed to identify that the bottom of the car had been cleaned. He identified several areas where there should have been dust, oil, or some sort of other coating such as dirt. It appeared that the bottom of the car had been cleaned and then moved to its new location. Xander agreed that the brown stain had a high probability of being blood. His uncertainty was where the blood came from. Was it from dropping the car on the Redwood killer? Or was it from someone cutting themselves while trying to clean the bottom of the car? The question I would posit is why would you clean the bottom of the car if not removing evidence of something you did not want to be found?

While what we had found certainly raised more questions than answers we could not find anything else of any significance in the junkyard. We unanimously agreed to move into the forest following the direction of the farm. We would not reach the farm before it was dark, and we thought it too dangerous to continue on in the black of the forest. If there was a danger lurking near that farm it would surely have the advantage over us at night. As we began to leave the junkyard, Laura stopped and looked as though she had seen a ghost. We all looked at her and I followed her eyeline toward one of the piles of metal. Visible was a number plate. That number plate was of the Range Rover that Sarah and her friends had arrived in. The car that had mysteriously gone missing three years earlier was in the junkyard next to the local village. We could not get up to the car itself but from the features we could make out it was clear to us that this was the Range Rover. It was also clear to us that the Fiat would probably be in one of the piles of metal around us also. However, there was no value in searching for it as there was no evidence to be found there other than evidence of a cover up. I could feel my anger rising and I could see Laura's. We had to focus and get to the farm. I wanted to speak to Laura, but she was not interested in hearing what I had to say. She understood the need to keep moving and did so without being asked. It was always better to try and follow Laura when she was like this than to try and lead her.

We walked along the track Pamela described, it was the clearest route to take us where we needed to go. We knew after about a mile we were going to have to veer off into the forest and head north. Another half mile into the forest there would be a clearing where we could camp for the night. We would be able to make it before dark and get set up and settled. Gus had improvised some traps to lay around the camp just in case the bogeyman came knocking. We were willing to take the risk of another group of campers approaching us in the night. Better they fall into one of our traps then we fall into the killer's hands.

We set up our camp and fire and sat in mostly silence for the first hour. We ate our food knowing that the next day was going to be a trek into the unknown and a search around an abandoned farm. My hope was the Pamela's story was not fabricated, but at the same time I was not so keen to come face to face with a seven-foot killer at this point. Over the previous three years I had gone over in my head what I would do if I ever met the person responsible for Sarah's disappearance. It always ended only one way violence. To me it was inevitable that I was going to take the life of the person that took Sarah from me. If we came face to face with him tomorrow any one of us could be the person that takes the fatal shot. For my closure I needed the executioner to be me.

When conversation did begin, it was disjointed at first. We discussed what we had found and what we had not found at the junkyard. Had the owner of the junkyard known those vehicles had come from missing persons? For how many years had the residents being taken abandoned vehicles to the junkyard to hide the evidence of evil misdeeds in the forest? Were the police involved in the cover up or did they just ignore it? Had we asked Xander three years ago if he thought the police could be involved in such an elaborate conspiracy, I'm sure he would have said no. The last three years had opened his eyes to the corruption of the local force. He had been hounded out not just because of him helping investigate Sarah's disappearance but because he would not blindly follow what his superiors told him. They actively discouraged investigation into large numbers of missing people. Xander never found out why. The chatter turned toward what we may face the following day. Gus gently flirted with Jennifer, suggesting that should he face a seven-foot monster tomorrow tonight should be all about pleasure. Jennifer had the read of Gus and knew that his banter was playful and harmless. While others may take sexual advances as harassment Jennifer knew there was nothing behind Gus's bravado. He did it purely for his own amusement and to try and make others smile. That was ignoring the fact that Jennifer was beautiful, and Gus was Gus.

I was keen to settle down for the night knowing that it would be difficult to get to sleep. The more I thought about it the less likely I was to sleep so the best plan I has was to get my head down early. The rest of the group were still buzzing with energy and Liam thought it best to produce a bottle of fireball whiskey for consumption. Normally I would discourage such behaviour, especially with the trek ahead of us, but I was aware that if there is a killer who's been roaming the forest for forty years we may not all make it through the next day. If some have a headache when they meet the devil that is their choice to make.

I awoke early the next day as the sun rose over the trees. I was the first to emerge from my tent. It seemed all others, including Laura and Gus, had partaken in the fireball whiskey. I half expected to see Jennifer come out of Gus's tent but unfortunately for the big man it was not to be. Jennifer was second to rise shortly followed by Laura. The remainder of the group then emerged, all but Gus. There were few bleary eyes, but nobody seemed particularly worse for wear. The fireball whiskey bottle was empty beside the dwindled fire. I found it strange that Gus had not emerged from his tent. Being a former military man, I expected a better level of discipline from him than the others, but his kind nature made it difficult to stay mad at him. I stood at his tent entrance raising my voice, but not to the level of a shout. Nothing. I got louder and looked at the group who looked back with an element of concern. Gus, normally so reliable, was not responding. I unzipped his tent and pick my head inside to see an empty space. He was not in his tent.

It was at this point an element of panic set in the group. Gus was, to the naked eye, the most dangerous of all of us. If he had been taken so quietly in the night, the rest of us had no chance of survival. We started shouting, echoes of his name rang round the forest. Abruptly we heard tree branches breaking behind us. Laura turned quickly, with gun in hand, to see Gus carrying a toilet roll under one arm and a Playboy under the other.

"Can't a man shit in peace?" he said.

He smiled, amused at himself. The rest of us were less amused but as the panic began to leave a few smiles appeared. It seemed Gus had woken early to check the traps around the camp. He wanted to see if any had been triggered by either animal or person. None had been disturbed. He had then taken the opportunity to follow his normal morning routine. We appreciated the distance he had gone from the camp to complete his business, we could not imagine anything nice coming out of a gentleman of his size. Gus and Laura took the traps down and piled them in the corner. It was suggested we leave them at the site as we would be returning that evening for rest. No need to carry more than we needed. We had discussed leaving the camping equipment also but decided previously to take them with us. To this day I do not know what motivated us to change our minds, but we decided to leave the camping equipment where it was. There seemed little value to take it with us and it would do nothing but add weight and slow us down. In all our trips into the forest over the previous year's none of us had ever come across another group. It was unlikely that anyone was going to stumble across our camp and, in the unlikely event that they did, they were not likely to want to steal anything. There was nothing of any real value.

We made our way towards the farm expecting to take at least two hours to reach our destination. Although not far as the crow flies, the terrain was difficult to navigate. How Pamela made it from the farm to the junkyard without breaking an ankle or falling off a cliff edge I do not know. It is testament to her mental and physical strength that she made it so far. We crossed streams, climbed hills, and avoided treacherous drops. The farm was elevated around six hundred to seven hundred feet higher than the campsite. For the most part the walk was comfortable however there were numerous spots where it was steep with loose rocks beneath your feet. The sun was high in the sky as we approached the farm. We could see darker clouds in the distance, the forecast had been for changeable weather but that was nothing unusual in this area. As we approached the farmhouse we slowed to take in the local area and identify any signs of life. We could see none. The area seemed as abandoned as any area could be. We agreed to scout the outside in two groups. There were seven of us and we decided that Laura would lead one group and Gus the other. I went with Gus, Liam, and Jennifer. The other group consisted of Laura, Damien and Xander. One group went left, the other group went right with the agreement to meet on the other side of the farm. We were not to stop for anything. If we saw something of interest, we had to note the location, regroup, and move there together as one unit.

As Gus let us around the right-hand side of the farm I took the rear position to ensure that Jennifer and Liam were between us. As we made our way around the building, we could see through the cracks in the wall darkness penetrated by streams of light coming in from holes in the roof. There were no signs of life in the derelict building. Liam had his camera ready, his role in the group was to document what we found. We wanted to photograph of any evidence that we found but not remove it. We did not want to be the reason that any official investigation failed. As we neared the meeting point with the other group, we came across a familiar sight; at least familiar for me. Lying near the entrance of one of the derelict buildings was a fully grown black and white cow. The cow had been mutilated in a similar manner to the sheep I had seen three years earlier. Liam photographed between gagging. I could not understand who could do such a thing to such a large creature. Gus added to Liam's fear by pointing out it looked like the cow had been dragged or partially carried from one of the nearby fields. Fully grown heifer could weigh almost a tonne. Whatever dragged that weight was stronger the most human beings. If not all human beings.

We rendezvoused with the other group a few minutes later. They had found nothing of any significance, but they had seen the old dwelling house Pamela described. We walked them round to the mutilated cattle. After everyone's shock and disgust settled down, we agreed that this was probably the perfect entry point into the building. The dead cow had not been there for long, decomposition had barely sat in. We could see Jennifer deep in thought. It was obvious she was trying to figure out what in the human psyche would drive somebody to such extreme lengths of violence. Her observations were intriguing.

Jennifer explained to us that most serial killers had sexual motivation towards their victims. For most of us sexual infatuation end in either lover's tryst or selfself-pleasure. The unnatural escalation of sexual feelings is generally accepted as stalking, then rape and finally murder. The murder acts, for the killer, as a release that they cannot get from what we would consider normal sexual activity. In this case, however, Jennifer did not think there was a sexual motive to the murders. With the history and legends, combined with the animal mutilations, she thought this more likely to be induced by some sort of uncontrollable rage. Anger not just at the world but at the living. This anger extended beyond the human species and the killer would likely see any living creatures' prey. The curious part for Jennifer was why not every living creature that entered the forest was murdered. In a rage this intense usually everything will be a target. The only way to stop the murder would be to stop the killer. There were documented periods of entry and exit of the forest without incident. Jennifer could see no pattern in when or where within the forest people went missing. The controlled nature of any crime scene clean-up also went against Jennifer's rage theory. While she acknowledged this, she reminded us that no profile is ever perfect. With every case they learn more and build more complex models. If we were to ever truly understand the human psyche, she believed it would probably drive one to taking their own life.

We entered the derelict building, passing the smelling, sticky corpse the cow. Immediately we found darkness. After a few minutes, our eyes began to adjust but we had no choice but to use our flashlights to see any detail within the building. We were in a large stone barn. We could see several doors and entrances along the right-hand side of the building. These either led to areas for cattle storage, equipment storage or pathways through the other buildings. We had no intention of splitting up, so we had to decide which door we tried first. It was agreed that the door farthest from us was probably the one that was going to take us deeper into the maze. From the outside these buildings seemed of standard size and shape. However, a quirk of the area meant the interior of the buildings were the opposite of the exterior. Where you expected walls there were none, where you expected open space there were doors and walls. We made our way to the last door and hesitated before opening it. As I was about to place my hand onto the handle Gus stopped me. He looked up and down at the other doors and decided the best option be to open them one by one.

I never liked my logic to be questioned but I thought I would give Gus a chance to explain his thinking before I said no. He pointed out that in his experience you were more likely to close a door than to leave it open. If we left all the doors closed and somebody else walked through them, they would likely close it behind themselves. If we opened all the doors an individual would still be likely to close it behind them. This would tell us if anybody had moved through the building other than us. I must admit it was an excellent idea. It also allowed us visual access to the layout of the building, to build a picture of the maze in our heads. Gus, Laura and Liam moved to the door nearest the entrance. One by one they opened the doors to mostly empty rooms or tight passageways to other parts of the building. There was nothing behind any of the doors of interest, so we continued with our original plan of going through the final door. Tentatively I opened the door and shone my torch. It was getting darker the deeper we went. I tried to think how anybody could have escaped in such darkness. I realised that perhaps at some point there may have been electricity running through this farm but no more. We could see rudimentary light bulbs and wiring across the roof of the building. There was however little chance that the electricity was still working. Nevertheless, Liam decided to try and flick a switch. Nothing. We continued through the labyrinth of the building wondering how Pamela ever made it out alive. There were no sounds but a lingering smell of damp, a musky, testosterone like smell.

We entered a large chamber like room in the

middle of which was an old wooden table. There was farm equipment from the 1930s and 1940s strewn around, none of which looked like it had been disturbed in many years. There was, however, a clear and well-worn path to the table. Around the table there were several broken glass jars, the contents of which had been removed prior to being broken. We followed the trail of glass jars around the table with our torches. As our torches settled on the table there was another unsettling sight before us. The table ahead was dark with blood. It would not be unusual for a table of this type in a farm outbuilding to have blood on it. I would imagine when they are killing pheasants or other game for eating this is where they would pluck and behead them. However, this farm and not been in use for many years, and while the blood was dry it still had an odour to it which was sickening. Liam tried to photograph the table; with the darkness the quality was going to be poor. Even with the flash there is only so much detail a camera can capture in the dark. Xander, ever the investigator, shone his torch into every nook and cranny in that room. We could find no evidence of any weapon or implement that had been used to kill. All the old farm equipment was dusty and had not been moved in many years. Whatever had been here had cleared itself out.

We continued our search around the outbuildings however could not find anything substantial other than the table in the middle of the room. The building matched the description Pamela had given to the police, both in its exterior architecture and his interior labyrinth. While the buildings were not particularly large, the combination of odd layout and darkness made it feel much bigger than it was. As we searched, we could find fresh evidence of sharp implements damaging wooden beams. We had seen nothing in our search they would be capable of doing such damage. It looked as though it had been an axe or some other exceptionally sharp, heavy cutting implement. Something had happened in this building. I was convinced we had found the lair of the Redwood killer.

We all felt unsettled about what we had found, between the mutilated carcass and the blood coated table. None of us wanted to speak about it. We wanted to hold it until we were back at the cottage, in an environment that felt safe and comfortable. We trekked back expecting to make the campsite before dark. The journey back was slower than the journey out. Imagining what could have been in the farm had exhausted us. We were also wary of our surroundings, more so than on our trek in. Every noise, every movement caused by the winds caught our attention. As we approached where we left our equipment, we were all looking forward to something to eat, something strong to drink and some rest. Gus was going to set the traps out again and perhaps fashion some more. It was clear he was moving into protective mode. He was a leader in every sense of the word yet still took an element of direction from Laura. We arrived at the campsite to find all our equipment and traps gone. Somebody had removed evidence that we had never been here.

Anger is the one word that I would use to describe the mood that came over the group at that point. We made the decision not to carry the equipment with us because of the speed at which we wanted to move. It struck all of us a little odd that, of all parts of the forest and of all days, somebody had come across our campsite. This could not have been a coincidence. I do not believe in coincidence. Gus and Laura both led a group each to look for our equipment, but we knew that we had no chance of finding it. Whoever had come through this area had meticulously covered any tracks that we had left. Evidence of the fire had been removed and the forest floor had been set to look like nobody had been through here in weeks. It was almost professional in its execution. After a short period of searching we had no choice but to continue to head back to the junkyard. We could not stay here at night, especially with bad weather rolling in from the north. We had a few hours of trek back to the junkyard, but it would be dark soon. It would almost certainly slow us down. Within twenty minutes of leaving the campsite the heavens opened and the rains poured down on us. We were prepared for bad weather but still did not want to be exposed to the elements. The wind picked up which made the rain come in at an odd angle. When it rained in this area the rain was cold, penetrating your skin and settling on your bones. Despite our excellent equipment we were getting soaked to our very core. As the weather worsened, we found ourselves more and more of danger of injury. There was not a clear path through the forest, so we had to step over branches, avoid puddles and cross ever increasing streams. Liam was the first to fall, spraining his ankle as he slipped on the log we had to cross. Now he was in a significant amount of pain, but he knew he had to continue. There was a good chance he had torn the tendons in his ankle. The good news was that shortly after his body began to react to the pain signals and numb the area. He described it as a mixture of warm on the outside and cold on the inside. Likely that was the swelling constricting blood vessels. We knew we had to keep going to the junkyard, but we also knew he could not continue to put full weight on the ankle for fear of damaging it further. Gus slowed, providing support for Liam so he did not have to bear his full weight on his ankle. He motioned to us to continue apace and they would meet us at the junkyard, but we were not going to split up. We were a team, and we were in this together.

We eventually got back to the junkyard, cold, shivering, and hungry. To our delight our van was still there. We helped Liam into it and got ourselves in. Gus started the engine and cranked up the heat. It would take a few moments for the engine to heat the air coming into the car. Gus hit the headlights and drove us out of the junkyard. We drove down the narrow winding road into the village. As we drove through the village, we noticed an unusual number of locals out on the street watching us pass. This was not a pleasant evening to be standing outside and it gave the impression that this was a warning not to come back. Suddenly Laura demanded we stop the van. Gus hit the brakes harder than he intended to and we all had a good jerk forward. We were about fifteen yards from the pub and the locals were still standing outside. Laura exited the van and Gus and I followed, instructing everybody else to stay put. Liam was not going anywhere, and Damian stayed with him. Xander and Jennifer, however, followed us into the pub.

Laura marched into the pub looking for any familiar face from her last visit. She found it with the younger police officer who had been so obstructive to our investigation. He was at a table with friends and they were laughing and joking and glancing toward us. She approached the table and confronted them. She explained about our missing equipment and how somebody who knew the area must have gone through and picked it up. They were dismissive of her and continued laughing and drinking. That was possibly the worst idea they had up until that point in their lives. Laura walked across to the bar and ordered pint of the horrid local brew. The barmaid, who was different from the last time we visited, looked at the young officer and he nodded and smiled.

"That one's on me Little Miss" said a gruff looking man who sat with the young officer.

"You have no idea how right you are" Laura said.

Laura approached the table, looked the man dead in the eye and poured the beer over his head. He stood up with such force that knocked the table over. Gus took one step forward, but I put my hand on his chest and motioned for him to stay. He looked at me and I smiled. He was close enough that if Laura needed him, he could be of help in an instant. But he was also far enough away that they did not see him as a threat yet.

"I'm not above hitting a lady" the man said as he puffed his chest and tried his best to appear intimidating.

"And I'm not above beating you into the 21st century" Laura replied.

Angrily the man clenched his fist and swung his right arm towards Laura. With ease she avoided his punch, grabbed his arm on the follow through and twisted the wrist upward forcing the man down onto one knee. With this came the warning that she would break his wrist without conscience. Clearly embarrassed the man continued his hate speech towards Laura, using words that I cannot type in a book to describe her. Most of the other locals had cleared a space conscious of Gus's presence. The young officer and his friend advanced on Laura. She gave them one more warning, all it would take was a step in the wrong direction and she would break his wrist. The young officer did not take heed of this warning. He moved not even an inch and there was a snapping sound and a scream of pain. Laura released the man's arm and he fell to the ground holding his wrist. His hand hung unnaturally to the side and he had turned as white as a ghost. His screams of pain must have been heard across the village. The young officer advanced and Laura struck him once with an open palm to the throat. He fell to both knees in front of her gasping for air as the third man moved. Gus quickly intercepted, grabbing him both hands round the throat and lifting him off his feet. Gus threw the man backward, through one of the tables. There looked to be others in the crowd who wanted to try their luck against Laura and Gus. Nobody wanted to go first, however. A familiar voice came from the front door. It was Henry, the senior officer in the area. He told the residents to stand down. When no one listened, he repeated his warning, adding that attention was not what the village was looking for and if anything were to kick off in the pub, attention is surely what would be brought. The locals backed off and Henry asked us to leave the pub. It was clear despite our suspicions of foul play we were not going to get anywhere. Laura had made her point, and we left the pub without further incident.

Henry let us know that if we left the village and did not return no charges were pressed. These were terms we could not fully agree to, so I offered a counterproposal. If we could travel through the village to search the forest without being stopped or harassed by the locals, we would neither press charges nor assault any other unsuspecting villagers. After a sigh and a roll of the eyes Henry accepted my proposal. Lauren and Gus got back in the van and I started to walk to join them. I turned to Henry and let him know we really did not want any further trouble. I also told him not to underestimate my resolve and finding the truth of what happened to my daughter.

# CHAPTER 20

Our loss of equipment slowed us down but it did not stop us. Being a man of deep pockets, I could quickly replace the equipment without worry of the cost. My biggest concern was the morale of the group. There was no doubt we had found something concerning but we did not really have solid evidence yet. Still, we decided to take the photographs of what we had found to the police. Xander assured us it was enough for them to begin at least a rudimentary investigation. We knew interest in the story would still be there because of Pamela and we could use that as leverage against the police. They did not want to be seen to be obstructing a civilian investigation into missing family. There would be too many questions as to why the police themselves were not doing more.

The next morning Laura, Xander and myself headed into the police station while Damien and Gus took my money to replace our stolen equipment. Arriving at the police station I could see the difficulty and disappointment in Xander's eyes.

He had given his life to the police and they had cast him aside as if he were nothing. When he eventually accepted his professional fate, he then lost his wife. There is no doubt this was going to bring back painful memories, but Xander's resolve was strong. He was a truth seeker in the truest sense of the words. His knowledge of the police hierarchy allowed us to see somebody senior immediately. The threat of the noise we could make around this did us no harm either. We quickly got access to a very senior regional police official. We shared what we had found but the poor quality photographs did not do service to the sight of the table coated in blood. However, it was enough for the senior officer to agree to investigate. He would send a team out there tomorrow to investigate what we had found. We shared our experience over camping equipment being removed and urged him to move faster. There was a cover up, one which we suspect he was a part of, and we did not want time to be wasted. However, with the officers available and the time remaining in the day they were better prepared to reach the site the next day. They were not looking to camp; their intention was to drive as close as possible before continuing on foot. At one point there would have been a track leading up to the old farm however over the years it would have grown over with trees bushes and grass. The farm had been abandoned for at least thirty years. We pressed further and insisted that at least Xander and me should accompany the police. Immediately the senior officer in front of us declined. We were not going to back down on this, however. We wanted to be there when the police found the site of a possible Redwood massacre. The officer asked for a moment alone clearly, he was contacting somebody. We stepped outside but left the door ajar. We listened as he relayed our story to whoever was on the end of the phone. There were lots of 'yes' statements and it was clear he was taking instructions and he 'understood'. He asked us to come back into the room and said that we could join him if we promised not to interfere or cause a ruckus. We were always going to agree, whether we intended to keep the promise or not.

Gus and Damien returned with new equipment arguably better than the equipment we originally had. My concern of cost was non-existent I could afford whatever we needed for as long as we needed it to be. We could not afford to lose any more days so it was agreed that while Xander and I were with the police, Gus and Laura would continue the search in other parts of the forest. We had a plan for the next day and I was certain that at the very least the police could not ignore what we found. I had not learned my lesson on hope yet, but it was coming soon.

We met the police at the junkyard the next morning. We had agreed that meeting in the village would be viewed as nothing other than antagonistic to the locals. Not that this bothered me, the locals had been nothing but obstructive in my search for Sarah. To me they were as guilty as any blood covered hands. Nevertheless, I wanted to keep the police onside for as long as I could. I was not a popular man with the police in this area, possibly only slightly more popular with them than I was in the village. Over the years there has been a turnover of some senior officers and my hope was that whatever was rotten in the regional police force had been identified and exorcised. If they could get rid of upstanding officers like Xander, surely they could get rid of the bad apples.

From the junkyard we took a police force truck up the track as far as we could. From there we were about a four hour hike up to the old farm. It was still early, and we had plenty of time. We should make it to the farm by lunchtime. The senior officer assured us that if we found anything, they would be able to make contact from their satellite phone and bring a helicopter in with forensic reinforcements. At that point, the helicopter would take myself and Xander back out of the area. Again, I did not argue but in my head I was convinced that they would not move me, regardless of what they tried.

Although the farm was elevated on a hill, the height of the forest and the local topography meant you could not see it until you were relatively close. What we could see as we approached however was smoke.

I felt a shudder go down my spine. I turned to Xander and the look on his face told me he was thinking the same as me.

"The bastard's burnt it down".

Xander I picked up the pace, not that it made much difference on this terrain. The police followed and as we got to the clearing a few hundred yards from the farm we could see the smouldering wreck of the buildings we had investigated the day before. We approached and could still see the red-hot burning embers. Although largely made of stone these old farm outbuildings had a core of wooden beams throughout. Once the wood burned the structural integrity of the roofs and the walls would weaken, and they would eventually cave in. The evidence we were wanting the police to examine was burnt. Up in smoke, as so much of my investigation had been. The entrance where the mutilated cow sat was clear. There is no sign of any such aberration. I could see the annoyance in the senior officer's face, he felt we had wasted his time. The irony was the phone call he made likely tipped off whoever came up to the farm to burn it down.

I was distraught. At every turn somebody was trying to stop me from finding the truth about Sarah. She was my world and had been torn from me. I felt in that moment that I was never going to find the culprit. I was now convinced more than ever there was a larger conspiracy at play. Whatever was happening at Redwood was happening with the tacit approval of the villagers and the regional authorities. The either knew what horror the woods contained or felt that it was not something they could control if they ever found it. Instead they let countless people enter the forest to never come home. They let countless families suffer deep devastating loss. They may as well have murdered Sarah themselves.

Xander placed his hand on my shoulder whispered some words in my ear and we slowly walked away from the police officers. Out with ear short of the local force Xander shared a theory with me. This part of the forest was too close to the edge to be the base for so many potential murders. Either the killer was nomadic and moved around the forest without pattern or he identified his targets, followed them, and killed them at the most appropriate spot. Either way it helped persuade me there were going to be more tables more cows and more evidence.

We had another two days before Gus and Laura led the group back to the cottage. Whatever was in the forest scared me. I do not mind admitting fear. If you do not have fear of such horror you are a fool. I might have been scared but I would never back down. I understood the danger which we were facing each time we stepped into the Redwood forest. This made waiting a nervous time. I knew that Gus and Laura could take care of themselves and protect the group under normal circumstances, but this was a situation none of us had faced before. We passed the time with a combination of research conversation, sleep, and alcohol. David had erected several boards in the cottage where he was tracking our locations, where was searched and where the last known positions of many of the missing people had been. Gus and Laura were searching the second farm on the list. With any luck they would have found evidence of something at that location. All we could do was way to return and hope that they were okay.

Laura, Gus, and the team returned with disappointing news. The second farm was in far worse condition than the first. There was no evidence that it had been used for anything recently. The run-down state of the farm indicated that it was dormant for many years. There was no question that somebody had sabotaged the second farmer as they had the first. The second farm had been sabotaged many years ago. Our two most likely locations for Redwood killer had thrown up a promising then disappointing result. I was convinced he would have been found at least at one of these farms, but where he had gone, we had no idea. Any evidence of his existence had been wiped in the fire. Each route we investigated was going to bring a lower probability of success.

Our next search was going to start at the main car park for the forest. Our hope was that the weather would discourage anybody else from coming out. It did. Our next three searches were going to emanate from this point, and we did not want to be explaining our presence to other people. There was also the question of accountability. If we met people in this car park and they entered the forest and never came back where we as culpable as the villagers nearby?

Our next two searches were uneventful and fruitless. All we succeeded in doing was lowering our morale and dwindling our energy. By this point you could see the fatigue setting in with Xander and Liam. This was not so much of physical fatigue as a mental fatigue. Investing yourself so deeply into this investigation had its consequences. You began to re-evaluate your obsession. I had the most to gain from finding the truth. As close as Gus was to his friends, Sarah was my one and only pride and joy. Liam's search was more out of obligation than emotion; he felt he owed it to his parents whom he barely remembered. If anybody were going to endure it would be me and I would carry the group kicking and screaming if I had to. They were my best bet at finding out what happened to Sarah.

# CHAPTER 21

By this point we had searched half the routes that we intended to. Our success rate was zero and our morale was following suit. We needed something to inspire and motivate us. I am not proud of what I did next nor am I proud of the consequences of my actions. I will have to live with them for the rest of my life, but to this day I feel it was my only chance to keep us driven forward. Frustration in the group was growing. Normally we got on very well, but strains were beginning to show. The only one who seemed immune to conflict within the group was Gus.

My intellect and ambition had often resulted in me being on the wrong side of an argument. Although I could never back down when I knew I was right, I did recognise the impact my obsession was having on the group. Even when I tried to simplify things for them, they could not always agree with my point of view. This was beginning to cause arguments, along with a breakdown in the relationship between Xander and Damien. Both men were exceptionally good people but Xander was meticulous and detail oriented in his action and Damien was more likely to listen to his gut. Xander wanted to continue the search as planned, Damien's belief was to go from the outside back in. He believed we should take our last planned search and do it next, then work backward.

Beyond the decision about which search to do next we needed something to unify the group again. I made my excuses to go out and get some fresh air and while there I placed an anonymous phone call through receptionist in the village hotel. I asked her to pass the message on to the young police officer in the village that the troublesome group of snoopers were going to be at the forest car park at 7:00 AM tomorrow morning. I told her that they intended search the forest for three more days and then start a search of the village. I wanted him to know they were blaming the villagers for the deaths and disappearances and were convinced that someone amongst the local community was the killer.

I re-entered entered the cottage to catch the start of a heated debate regarding our next move. I reminded everybody of why we were here, what we had to gain and what we had to lose. I helped them remember that the local community and authorities wanted us to fail. With that, I threw my support behind Damien's recommendation. Do the unexpected, I thought, and you may achieve unexpected results. I assured Xander that if tomorrow's search were wholly unsuccessful, we would revert to the original plan. However, if there was any sign of the Redwood killer, we would continue with Damien's approach. That settled the debate for the evening but there was still tension in the air.

This was not my area of expertise. Usually when I wanted something, I just demanded it and I could not demand of this group any more than they were already giving without losing their help. I had to rely on Laura and Gus, which was not a natural state for me. The answer seemed to be at the bottom of a bottle of tequila. We had an early start again in the morning, but after tomorrow I knew we would be united once more.

The previous day's arguments weighed heavy on us the following morning. The drive to the forest was in almost complete silence, which was only punctuated when we arrived to see a group of young men from the village awaiting us. There were about seven of them and two of them were brandishing shotguns. One of the group was the young police officer from the village, although he was not wearing his uniform. My manufactured confrontation had begun.

Gus and Laura took centre stage, standing in front of the rest of the group demanding to know what was going on. The young officer, wary of being injured as his friend had been a few nights earlier, instructed them to stay where they were lest they be shot. Threatening Gus is never a good idea. It was at this point he dropped his bag to the ground reached in it and pulled out Big Bubba, his heavy machine gun. Although well aged Gus had maintained the weapon perfectly and it would fire off several rounds before either shotgun could be raised in anger.

"We can play if you want to play" Gus exulted.

It was at this point I wanted Liam to take a photograph of the villagers faces, however he was back at the cottage, still on the side-line due to his injured ankle. The villagers had never seen such a weapon before, although they realised that this would be a losing fight if it started. After a tense standoff there was agreement by both groups to put their guns down and to the side. Laura tried to negotiate with the group. She told them that if they let us pass and we found nothing on this next search we would not come back. I tried to interrupt; I would not agree to these terms but Laura shot me down immediately. From the look on her face it was clear her patience had gone. She was ready for a confrontation whether it be with me or with a group of villagers. Considering my options, I decided to let her approach play out.

To my internal delight the group turned Laura's offer down. While there was not a significant difference in the numbers between the two groups, most of the villagers were considerably younger and in better shape than us. Xander I suspect it would be able to hold his own, Gus and Laura would have no problems protecting themselves. Damien was clearly in shape and would last well in a fight. I knew I could handle myself if it came to it, however I was not as young as I used to be. It had been many years since I had raised my hands in anger.

I would accept whatever beating came my way to pull this group together. Before the morning descended into a scene from West Side Story, Henry arrived in the local police car. He got out, dressed in full uniform, and began to try to talk us down. This confrontation was only going to end one way and it was going to be in violence. The level of the violence with the villagers bringing their shotguns could have escalated but, with those now cast aside, the worst that was going to happen were some bruises and broken bones. Henry was unlikely to convince either group to stop.

One of the group from the village approached Laura. He towered above her but then her stature was never that great. He had to have been aware of what happened to the villager in the pub but, rather foolishly, he did not seem intimidated in the slightest. Henry continued to approach the two groups trying to get our attention. The villager used this distraction to lunge at Laura. Without missing a beat Laura sidestepped him, raised her arm, and struck the villager forcefully in his face with her elbow. He went down quickly, rolling around holding his face. Through his fingers you could see the blood beginning to seep. One of the larger villagers decided he wanted to try and take down Gus. As Gus was distracted and laughing watching Laura's latest victim squirming on the ground, the man sucker punched him from the side. The villagers face was immediately wracked with pain. He grabbed his wrist having injured his hand on Gus's hard head. No one had taught the man how to throw a punch. Gus showed less pain and more annoyance. He turned to the villager, looked him straight in the eye and headbutted him. You heard the crunch of the villager's nose as it broke and he hit the ground almost as fast as Laura's attacker.

By this time Henry had reached both groups. The villagers had realised that regardless of the shape of the rest of my team they, were no match for Gus and Laura. It was at this point one of them reached for his shotgun. He grabbed it from the ground and started to raise it, hoping his aim was true. He was only going to get one shot at this. Henry grabbed the end of the shotgun and tried lower it to the ground again. There was a loud bang and scream of pain. The shotgun had gone off with its barrels aimed at Henry's legs.

With the proximity shotgun to Henry's legs, the damage was immense. Henry's right leg was almost completely detached above the knee. His left leg had significant trauma and damage. There was more blood than most of us had seen in our lives; it was like a scene from a horror movie. This was a time critical situation which I had not foreseen when I set up with the confrontation. Henry was severely injured and needed immediate medical attention. There was no phone reception and with a young officer being part of the group of villagers there was no one at the end of the radio in the police station. Gus rushed to Henry, treating the wound as best he could. He created a makeshift tourniquet for both legs to try and stem the blood loss. The villager who pulled the trigger was sat on the ground sobbing as his friends tried to assure him it was an accident. The young officer was panicking realizing his part in his friend's injury. No one knew that I was the architect of this disaster.

We rushed Henry into the police car and drove it aggressively to the village. As soon as there was phone reception an ambulance was called. Henry had no chance of survival if we had to drive him to the hospital, his chances were low enough in an ambulance. We took him to the police station and sent for the local doctor. He was able to administer some pain medication and apply more suitable tourniquet to Henry's legs. The pain medication kicked in. I had assumed it was the same medication given to me, however Henry did not pass out. He was conscious, if confused, but still had an element of discomfort. He had bravely battled the pain. Except for the initial scream upon being shot he had made virtually no noise on the journey back into the village. By some degree of luck there was an ambulance only twenty minutes away attending to another call. Deemed less critical than Henry's condition, the ambulance was left its current call and was re-directed to the village.

Upon arriving at the village police station, the paramedics were aghast at what they saw. Although injuries, even hunting accidents, were not uncommon in the area such damage was unseen. Henry was rushed to hospital and died on the table twice during operations. He lost both of his legs but, by the grace of God, survived his ordeal. I expected him to be filled with rage and spite.

Before writing this book, I spoke to Henry and admitted my part. Henry had forgiven us all a long time ago for what happened, and he was not surprised when I confessed. Henry shared with me that he felt a partial responsibility for what happened, not only on that day but with my daughter and the many other missing people. While he could never tell me why the disappearances were ignored, he did tell me that he felt losing his legs was the price he paid for his part in it. He shared that he always felt he would have to pay the ultimate price for his sins and at the end of the day not being able to walk but still being able to breathe air as a free man was a win.

# CHAPTER 22

My plan to unite the group backfired. The accident tore us apart. Laura and Gus had seen the horrors of war and were less affected by the others.

Xander realized the path we were on and the darkness that was at the end of it. He had been given a chance to rebuild his life after his wife died and, in his eyes, he thrown it away.

Damien felt huge guilt for what happened to Henry. He knew how the local villagers felt about our group entering the forest investigating their secrets. He said he should have foreseen the trouble and had he done so he would not have taken part, and Henry would not have lost his legs. I tried to assuage his guilt and convince him that he was not at fault. I could not tell him how I knew that to be true. Hopefully reading this he will gain some comfort to know that the burden sits solely with me.

David had known Henry for most of his life. After the shooting David's few remaining friends in the village refused to speak to him and he became withdrawn from society. He cut contact with almost everybody in the group except for Jennifer, for whom he had a soft spot. He continued to investigate instances of supernatural occurrences, but it was from the privacy of a darkened room in front of a computer. He is almost a complete hermit now and I worry that by having him as part of the group we damaged his already fragile mental health and ruined his life.

Gus, Laura, and Liam stayed with the group. Jennifer had to return to her day job as a criminal profiler. She stayed in touch and where she could she helped in deciphering the many legends to create a more accurate profile of our killer. She never published her analysis of the group however she did share with me that my narcissistic personality was likely to drive Laura farther away if I could not give up my obsession with finding Sarah.

Henry's accident had delayed us several weeks in our search. The police investigation, as with the investigations into the missing people, was not very thorough. They quickly wrote it off as a hunting accident and no charges were brought against the villager who pulled the trigger. In the villagers eyes the blame was clear. To them it was wholly our fault. They considered the damage their opposition had done, and we agreed that, while we would continue our investigation, we would not stop in the village or engage any resident. We never had any further problems with the villagers after that date, although we never stopped in the town limits to test the truce.

The four of us who remained carried out the final searches, but we found nothing. No evidence of a killer, no evidence of a murder. Gus and Laura both decided to carry on with their lives. I understood for Gus, he had carried his burden long enough. He assured me should anything ever change he would be there nothing would stop him from helping me. We stayed in contact over the years and he has always been a good friend.

I struggled with Laura's decision to stop looking for her sister. I never thought she would abandon her. Laura and I had many heated arguments during the following weeks about her decision to leave. The search for Sarah drove a further wedge between us. Laura could never accept my obsession with finding out what truly happened to her sister. She saw it as unhealthy and damaging and felt that I was using it as an excuse to not live my life. In anger, and out of hurt and spite, I called her a coward, even though deep down I know nothing is further from the truth. I have not seen Laura in five years and except for a twice-yearly phone call we never talk.

Only Liam stayed by my side. We continued searching for over a year. In that time, we covered less than 30% of the Redwood forest.

# CHAPTER 23

Despite the focused methodology in which we searched, Liam and I were getting nowhere at an increasingly fast pace. We had covered only a small section of the overall Redwood forest, but we felt we had hit all the key areas we could identify, the areas where we may find evidence of the Redwood killer. This was mentally and physically exhausting for both Liam and me. I was beginning to exhaust the funds I had available to continue the search and my desire to go back to work without answers was non-existent.

Liam had stood by me during this time without work and I was paying for both of us to live in the cottage for over a year. The strained relationship with my daughter, along with the isolation in the local area, was taking its toll on me. My feeling of uselessness was ever increasing. It seemed that no matter how hard I tried I could not make progress in my search for Sarah. Every day, I was failing again. It was now six years since Sarah's disappearance and two years since I did a day of paid work. I had fallen behind on my house payments and in the six years I had spent over one million dollars on my search. What little funds remained would only give us the opportunity for the search of one more area.

I had the difficult and heart wrenching decision to make around where our last search would take place. I knew this was the last roll of the dice and I could not afford for it to be snake eyes. We examined the map and the various locations which we had searched. There was only one habitable spot that we had not been. As we discussed our options, I was aware this would have been a near impossibility for the location of the Redwood killer. My suspicions about the nature of the evil which lurked in the forest were that he had no central structure from which he carried out his misdeeds. From what we had observed this was a nomadic monster. We had seen evidence of the killer near the junkyard, and this was also the area of the only confirmed sighting of him. However, when we examined the spate of killings over the years it was clear that they were random in pattern. I suspected that each was a kill of opportunity based on where the killer was resting at the time. This explained the time gap between murders; in such a large area the killer could lie dormant if no victims came close enough.

I took our final search pin and pushed it into the board. It was at the old military base. I knew that there were guards patrolling the area which would made access exceptionally difficult. I had previously contacted the Department of Defence for permission to carry out a walk across the grounds. It was denied. Although no longer in use, the area of land and the bunker which it contained was of significance to national security. At least, that is what the letter told me.

For this to be successful Liam and I would have to separate on a search for the very first time. In the ideal scenario two guards patrolling such a large area would give me ample opportunity to slip in unseen and look for any evidence. There was little chance that there would be evidence somewhere around on military property however each turn in the search had surprised us. The guards patrolled but were not on the lookout for subtle clues so if there was anything it would likely remain unfound. We would approach the area with caution and watch from a distance to see if we could ascertain the guard's patterns and behaviours. Should my plan of sneaking in unseen not look to be feasible, Liam would provide a distraction. He would be the lost hiker, cold, injured and looking for help. The guards would be unlikely to leave the property to help him, however he should provide enough distraction for me to get on the land and have sufficient time to investigate.

We were in the twilight of summer. That meant we would still have sufficient light to hike close to the base, but we would look to camp out of sight. We would be able to leave our equipment in a safe place. We had no issues with the villagers since Henry's accident and did not foresee any soon. This gave us approximately sixteen hours of sunlight with which to approach the military base and carry out rudimentary observations. We took enough provisions with us to ensure that should my search unearth any clues or evidence of the Redwood killer we would be able to camp an extra night and carry out a second search.

As we approached our campsite we saw, unsurprisingly, no evidence of the Redwood killer. We set up camp, ate the basic food we had brought with us and settled down for the night. To start far enough away from the base and hike close enough unseen had been a long hike on a particularly warm day. The evening pattern was the same now. Liam and I did not speak much on the hike. This was not because we were not getting along, it was merely we had spent so much time together small talk seemed unnecessary. We no longer felt the need to fill the silence with chatter. It did not help that Liam was still young and his interests greatly diverged from mine.

Liam was beginning to show strain from the searching, especially with the lack of results. He was becoming more withdrawn and struggling with the emotional guilt of his parent's untimely death. He had dedicated almost two years of his life to a fruitless search for his parent's killer. He had forgone further education and employment in an attempt to close that chapter of his life. Despite being a mature adult my inability to get to the truth made me feel like a failure. I can imagine that Liam did not feel too different from me, however I was not sure he had the required level of maturity to know how to carry such a burden.

Liam and I observed the bunker from the nearest tree line. We were still approximately one hundred yards from the gate and fence, at which point the land moved from public to military ownership. We watched for an hour as the guards patrolled the area and we could see no discernible pattern. We had expected two guards at the base however it soon became clear there were four. They worked in groups of two and, being military men, did not look so different from each other. This would have contributed to the belief it only two guards patrolled the area. Liam was going to need to be the distraction. He approached the main gate without his jacket or any equipment. He was to tell the two guards at the gate the story of his bad luck in losing his equipment in a fall. His jacket he had given to a friend in the forest to keep him warm while he went for help. Luckily, he had stumbled across the military base, or at least that was the tale he was going to tell. Prior to Liam approaching the gate, I walked the forest line as far as I could so that I was out of sight of any of the guards. The chain link fence should be easy to cut allow me access onto the property. From there I would use whatever cover available to move around the land. There was enough space that I should be able to avoid being spotted, and if necessary be able to hide from the guards.

The plan was foolish and desperate, but at this point I was a desperate man. If I were caught, I would get a slap on the wrist, perhaps even a police caution. If I were not caught, I would be able to cross off the last area we would be able to search. Had I found evidence of the Redwood killer on the military property I am not sure what I would have done with it. The police were involved in a cover up in the local area, but I was confident the military would be more receptive should there be a killer on their land. The chances were slim. Four armed guards at this juncture would indicate ad the Redwood killer been in this area they would likely have seen and killed such a monster or being killed themselves.

I cut the fence and entered as silently as I could. I needed to be out of sight of both Liam and the guards to be successful in infiltrating the land. The downside of this as I was not sure how well Liam was getting on with his distraction. I had to trust that he could play his part as well as required. I began making my way across the land looking for any evidence linked to the missing and murdered people. It was becoming clear after an hour of searching but this was going to be another unsuccessful hunt. There were clear open spaces all around me and I moved as stealthily as I could across the land. I used whatever natural cover I could, ensuring I did a three hundred and sixty degree observation before moving from cover. For an unused military base the land was well kept. The grass had been kept short, and bush and tree growth were mostly controlled. There was evidence of gunfire with some used shell casings littering a small area. It was clear that they had used the area for some shooting practice, with one of the walls peppered with bullet holes. In such a remote area you could get away with gunfire without arousing suspicion. This meant that they could practice their aim, whether they were supposed to or not.

The open space was quite vast, larger than it had looked on the map and was beautiful, if sparse. Along one edge of the military base was a wooded area. Instead of clearing this area as they had the rest, the military had built their fence in amongst the trees. This was no doubt advantageous for any training exercises over the years to have a wooded area protected from the public being available for war games. I made my way amongst the trees conscious that this was likely to be the last area I searched. I expected nothing.

As I moved through the woods, I became aware of some form of movement following me. I could see nothing, but my senses in these woods were now finely tuned to allow me to feel disturbances in the atmosphere. I could also hear the occasional rustling of leaves and branches breaking under the foot of something with considerable weight. This was not a rabbit or a deer. This was a human being. I had a mix of panic and excitement. I was not prepared to go head to head with the Redwood killer as our guns had returned with Gus. I did however have some things on my side, righteous anger, and the element of surprise. If the Redwood killer was following me, he would have no idea that I was aware of his presence. My thoughts shifted to how I would trap this monster. He arguably had the advantage knowing the forest so well. It occurred to me that with the forest blocking out a lot of sunlight I may be able to use one of the older broken trees as a distraction. I removed my jacket and placed it over a dead tree. In good light this would look nothing like a human being. In the shadowy undergrowth, however, it would look somewhat human, at least until you got fairly close. I moved as quietly as I could, slipping behind a nearby tree. I had no weapon but there were plenty thick branches covering the forest floor. I picked one up, confident I could swing it with enough force to take any monster off his feet. I could not peer round the tree to watch my stalkers approach. I was going to have to rely on my other senses. I closed my eyes and listened intently. Once I felt I was in tune with the forest I opened my eyes again. I knew what I was listening for, and when I heard it, I would strike.

He was getting ever closer. In a few moments I would pounce from behind and take him down. I focused on my breathing, keeping it slow and steady. I tightened my grip around the log in my hand. This was my moment. This was my retribution.

# CHAPTER 24

Just before I made my move, I felt cold metal press against the back of my head. There was an instruction not to move. All I could think was not now. I was so close. I could hear the monster approach. The soldier who held me at gunpoint had given our position away, to a ruthless serial killer no less. Before I had a chance to warn him our stalker appeared.

It was another guard. In my blinkered and narrowed mind, it had not occurred to me that I had been seen. There was no monster following me, only two military. They instructed me to release my grip of the log, which I did without argument. I would take my slap on the wrist without confrontation. They marched me out of the forest and, once we were on better terrain, they instructed me to put my hands behind my back and placed handcuffs around my wrists. The cuffs were tightened to painful degree. I tried to let them know over the pain I was in however they were not interested. This was not the local police I was dealing with. These men were trained to go into a warzone and deal with whatever came their way, with unflinching bravery. I was not going to be mistreated nor was I going to be treated with kid gloves.

They escorted me to the main gate where the two other guards were waiting. Liam was kneeled in front of them, also in handcuffs. It seemed our notoriety had alerted the military that we may try such a foolish stunt. They knew who we were the moment Liam approached the gate. All that remained was to find me on the land. That was not going to be a difficult task for well-trained soldiers.

Technically, Liam had not entered the military property without permission. They could see he was a scared young man and realised that what had happened thus far was probably punishment enough for him. One of the guards went to the command post, presumably to radio his superiors, and returned shortly after to release Liam. They forcibly escorted him to the gate and give him a gentle shove to the other side, closing the gate noisily behind him.

I was held outside on my knees for forty minutes. It was not until a military truck arrived that I was informed that I was allowed to stand. My hands felt slightly sticky, which I later realized was blood caused by the chafing of the handcuffs being too tight. Once the truck pulled up one of the rear doors was opened and I was bundled into the back of it. A hood was placed over my head and tightened around my throat. I could feel the rope pressing my gullet, however I could still comfortably breath. Nothing was said to me during this time. The truck left back down the road it had just come up. We drove for what seemed like forever, my best guess was that it was around two hours of travel. Still wearing my hood and unable to see anything I was taken from the truck and walked to a heavy metal door. I knew it was metal and heavy from the noise it made when it was opened. I was marched thirty steps forward and ten steps left. We entered a room and placed in a chair. I heard the door shut and my hood was removed.

Stood beside me was a guard and shining into my face was a bright lamp. I could not make out the shape or size of the room, the light in my eyes almost blinding. I asked the guard what was going on but there was no response. I tried to rise from my chair and the guard reacted. He put his hand on my shoulder and forcibly pushed me down. I tried to stand again and once more was pushed down by the soldier. The third time I tried to rise the guard put his hand on my shoulder, forced me down and made it clear that his other hand was now on his weapon. I am belligerent, and I recognise this personality trait, however this was not the time to continue my behaviour. I sat in silence with the guard stood next to me for an unknown amount of time. At this point I was disorientated thirsty and hungry. I had no idea how long I had been in this room, or how long I was going to be in this room. The door opened and a well-dressed older gentleman walked in. I could not see through the door he had entered. There was light coming in, but it did not illuminate the room enough to counteract the lamp that shone in my eyes. The man sat across from me and pulled out a recording device. I could not make out much of his facial features, my assumption is the lamp in my face was not there just for intimidation. It served the dual purpose of making me feel uncomfortable and hiding the identity of my interrogator. He asked for my personal details, name, address and so forth. I was certain they already knew who I was so there is no reason for me to try and hide it. I had told my story to the police, to the newspapers, and to the residents. I had no secrets to keep here.

Had I wanted to keep information to myself I doubt they would have had interrogation techniques sophisticated enough to work on someone with my mental strength. There was, however, no reason for me not to share why I was on the military property. I answered his questions honestly and sincerely. There were a number which made no sense to me. He asked me about my religious beliefs and whether I believed in God and the Devil. He asked me if I was superstitious man and whether I believed in the supernatural. It felt at times like they were trying to trap me in a psychological profile which would end with me in a straight jacket next to Pamela. I answer truthfully and let him know that I would be of no further nuisance to them. What I had seen on the military property had convinced me but there was no bogeyman, at least not in that part of the forest.

His last question was whether I had a high tolerance for physical pain. This was an odd and unsettling question. This was the military, and I was a civilian. Surely, they were not going to torture me. I answered truthfully, letting him know the physical torture would not work on me. With all I had been through over the years nothing could be worse than the pain I had already suffered. He left the room and again I sat with blinding light in my eyes with an unresponsive guard to my side. More time passed before another man entered the room. This time I could make out that he was wearing military uniform, although it looked to be that of a more senior officer. He explained to me the trespass on the base was a matter of national security. Therefore, they could hold me indefinitely without a lawyer or trial. They had to fully investigate my story before they released me, and I would be detained until they were satisfied. He let me know that the facility which I was in was one of the older bases in the area and not built for comfort. There were several military bases in the area that I could have been at.

The officer continued explaining to me that I

would be held until such time that my story was verified, and they could be sure that I was not a threat should I be released. I pleaded and tried to convince him that I was no such threat. I had learned my lesson, my search for Sarah had come to an end. He leaned forward blocking, some of the light from the lamp. For the first time I could see his face. He was a stern looking man and the insignia on his uniform indicated he was a high-ranking officer in the army. I was in serious trouble. He looked me straight in the eye with a steely gaze.

"You better hope that's true" he warned me.

The hood was placed back over my head and I was taken down what I can only assume was a hallway and placed into a bare room with a heavy metal door. The door had a slit in it at eye level which could be closed from the outside, used by the guards to see into the cell. There were no windows just grey, concrete wall. There was a hatch at the bottom of the door which I assumed was for putting food through. In the corner there was a plumbed toilet, although it did not look particularly comfortable nor hygienic. There was a concrete slab one foot off the floor with a thin mattress on top of it. Folded on the mattress were a blanket and a pillow. I was in for an uncomfortable night. Not long past before the slot at the bottom of the door was opened and a tray with food and a glass of water was pushed through. Surprisingly, the food was better than what local village pub served however the water, being at room temperature, was not brilliant. I could not wait for the next day to come, time for me to get back to the modern conveniences of the rented cottage.

# CHAPTER 25

I had no idea how much time had passed. There were no windows in the room I was held in and the lights were switched on and off randomly. I know I had been served over fifty meals, which appeared to be split in breakfast lunch dinner. That gave me the rough idea that I had been held for around two weeks, but I could not be sure. Like the lighting food distribution seemed almost random. I had no access to phone, a lawyer, or any modern conveniences. I had not brushed my teeth or washed for the entire time I was held. It was inhumane.

For the entirety of my captivity I had not spoken to another human being since the day I had been brought in. I could feel my sanity beginning to slip away. I feared my humanity would not be far behind it.

I tried to exercise as much as I could in the small room. It was no larger than nine feet by nine feet. I paced the room to keep my legs moving and did a mix of sit ups and press ups to try and maintain some core strength. There was little else I could do. I had nothing to read nor anything to watch.

Physical torture is outlawed under international law however this kind of mental torture seemed to be tolerated. The only thing that kept me going was the thought that I was still failing Sarah.

I was lying on the concrete slab bed when I heard that click of the lock in the door. It swung open and standing there was the guard had brought me in. I started to stand up and was abruptly told to sit back down. The guard entered and placed a hood over my head, handcuffing my hands behind my back. This time the handcuffs were loose fitting, not to the extent that I could release my hands but there was going to be no physical damage this time unless I struggled. I was walked out of the room and around the unknown building until I could feel the fresh air pass over my hands. I heard a car door open and was bundled into back seat, with the door slammed shut behind me. It was daylight, I could see changes in shade on the hood, but I had no idea of the time. After spending hours in the truck, we promptly stopped. I was taken out of the back of the vehicle and my handcuffs were removed, quickly followed by my hood. I was outside the village pub. I was wearing the same clothes as the day I was detained.

The guard handed me my phone, my wallet, and my watch. His face lacked any emotion or empathy for my situation. It did however give away that there was an unpleasant odour coming from me. I have never lived in such filth as I did during the time which I was detained. Without a word the guard got back in the military truck and the tinted passenger window went down. An older looking gentleman in a black suit white shirt and black tie stared at me.

"If we see you again, the instruction is to shoot on sight" he told me. With that the truck drove away and I was left standing looking and feeling like a homeless person. I stood on the side of the road in a village where I was no longer welcome.

I checked my phone. Of course, there was no charge left on the battery. My wallet had some cash in it, enough certainly to pay for a taxi back to the cottage. My only challenge was I had no way of contacting the taxi company. I stared at the pub entrance, wondering what reception I would get if I walked in. The village had no phone box anymore, and the library was the only other place that may allow me to make a call however it would be shut by this time. I took a deep breath and looked down at myself. I was filthy and smelly. I was also hungry and thirsty, but that would need to wait. If I was to venture into the lion's den, the pub, then it had to be quick. Make the call and get out. I lifted my head and strode through the door.

# CHAPTER 26

Immediately the pub went silent. The eyes trained on me were angry and judgemental. I had made the villagers lives more difficult through investigating Sarah's disappearance. This was their own fault. Had they been honest, had they helped fully, I would have had the truth and left a long time ago. At times I pitied their ignorance. In my darkest moments, their ability to ignore the suffering of others and only focus on their own selfish needs was something I envied. Most of the time, however, I was just disgusted by them. As bad as I smelled, they had a worse odour. They had the odour of conspiracy and murder.

As intense as they looked at me, I held my head high as I strode up to the bar. I could look angry too. I could judge them also. I stood at the bar waiting for the barmaid to put down the glass she was neurotically cleaning. Eventually she did so and then wandered closer to where I was waiting.

"You're not welcome here" she blurted out, bluntly.

I tried to explain my situation, and that all I

needed to do was call a taxi. She was having none of it. She repeated her statement, after which two larger men stood from their table. They walked slowly toward me. It occurred to me that they thought I may not be alone, that Gus and Laura might be with me. I could use that to my advantage.

"The three of us need a taxi, that is all." I said confidently.

The two men stopped dead in their tracks. The memory of Laura and Gus must still be fresh in the villager's minds. They told the barmaid to hand me the phone in a gruff and terse tone. She did so and I called my taxi. It would arrive in fifteen minutes. As along as I wasn't found to be alone, I was going to be fine. I quietly asked the taxi driver to pick me up outside the library. I did not want to be near the pub any longer than I had to.

Not wanting to stoop the villager's level I thanked that barmaid politely and left. As I exited two more men entered. The blocked my exit initially, however the two burly men who had thought of doing me harm indicated to let me past. I nodded as the men parted and quickly exited after squeezing between them. I walked faster upon exiting the pub. The library was not far, and I would be out of the view of most people. It was unlikely anybody of any threat would pass me there.

As I hurriedly walked away from the pub the two men who had just entered came back out. They looked my direction and put their hands in their pockets before walking in my direction. I was sure this was a coincidence however I did not want to take the chance. I carried on walking, not wanting to look over my shoulder and seem either suspicious or concerned. I walked another one hundred yards before turning down the next street in the direction of the library. As I turned, I glanced toward the pub. The two men were still following me and had closed the gap between us considerably. I Took a few hurried steps and then focused in front of me. It was as I picked up the pace two shapes emerged from the shadows. It was the two men who had cautiously approached me in the pub. It now became clear that the two men who entered had given up my secret that I was there alone.

I turned to go back the way I came but as I did so my followers appeared around the corner. I was trapped, and in no condition to run. The four men were clearly in better physical shape than me, and were likely well rested and well fed. I was not. I thought my superior intellect may get me out of the situation. It was certainly worth trying. I explained as the men approached what my predicament was, and that I had no intention of entering the village but was given no choice. I tried to clarify what the consequences would be if our unofficial truce were broken, that holy hellfire could reign down from my friends. They were unimpressed, and unmoved. I had already been caught fabricating my single status in the village. Even those as intelligence challenged as these men would correctly deduce there would be no cavalry.

I backed myself against the wall behind me. If I had any chance of defending myself, I had to be able to see all four men. They closed on me. I had never felt more like prey in my life. I was desperate, and desperate men are dangerous.

It did not matter how dangerous I was. There were four of them, physically strong and no doubt with far greater stamina than I had. In almost an old movie style one of them was rolling up their sleeves, another removing his jacket. It didn't look expensive, but he obviously did not want to get blood on it. One approached with pace. As he reached me I swung with all the power I could muster. I landed a clean punch across the side of his face. Although he stumbled, he did not fall. It clearly hurt him but not as much as I wanted or needed. Another moved forward and I jabbed with my left and hooked with my right. I was older but still had fast hands. Both strikes hit hard. This man did fall but only to one knee. Before I had time to reset myself there was an almighty thump to my temple. Everything flashed black as I crumpled to the ground. Had this been one on one, or even two one, I may have stood a chance. Four on one however were odds I could not win.

As I lay on the ground my instincts told me to get up. I began to rise, getting to one knee. I saw a brief flash of another fist coming down at me. The contact wasn't as clean as his first punch, but it made good contact around my orbital bone. There was a slight crack and my face hit the ground. I could taste blood and my eyesight was blurred. Without warning my body started jolting and I was feeling pressure and pain all over. The men were kicking me as I lay on the ground. I do not know how many blows I took, there was no point counting. I thought I was going to die at the hands, or feet, of only slightly evolved troglodytes. As suddenly as the kicks started, they stopped. I heard a voice demanding the men back away. The voice was one I recognised; it was the junior police officer.

After Henry's accident the junior officer was the only one left in the village. Henry was never replaced. The impact of the incident had weighed heavily on the junior officer. The silver lining of such incidents can be the change they cause in people. In this case the junior officer had matured and was far less volatile. He was almost a proper police officer, if you ignore the fact he was part of a conspiracy to cover up murder. At this point however he was my only defence from serious injury, or even death.

I heard a call for an ambulance and lay on the ground not moving until one arrived. It must have been almost an hour. Although there was no more violence against me, I lay there without cover or comfort. The officer could not leave my side lest the beating recommence and no-one else in the village was willing to help me. When the ambulance arrived, they carried out a quick initial assessment and rushed me into the ambulance. I was conscious and responsive, but they were concerned about unseen injuries. The ride to the hospital was long. I was in significant pain and I wondered how Henry tolerated the wait for help with the pain he must have been in.

Once we reached the hospital I fell in and out of consciousness as they ran tests and scans. Once I was fully awake I had found I had lost another few days. Thankfully, there were no serious injuries. This time when I awoke there was no-one at the hospital with me. I was completely alone. I had suffered a minor break to my orbital bone and another concussion. Due to the nature of the head injury and the fact it was my second serious concussion in a matter of years I was again to stay in for observation. With no threat from Laura hanging over my head I discharged myself that day. I left the hospital with a pocketful of tramadol and not much else, other than my now filthy and blood-stained clothing.

I called a taxi and when it came, despite the

look of disgust from the taxi driver, I got in and instructed him to take me straight to the cottage.

I entered the cottage to find it undisturbed. The only noticeable difference from when I had last been there was that all of Liam's possession had gone. I plugged my phone into charge, undressed and went straight into the shower. I must have spent at least twenty minutes washing myself, trying to remove not only the stench but the feeling of imprisonment. When I got out of the shower I went straight to my phone and turned it on. There were no messages and no missed calls. In some ways this was not a surprise. I communicated very little with any part of the outside world these days. I had hoped that Liam had left me a message to explain where he had gone but there was none. I tried calling him and text him several times, but his phone was always off. I did not hear anything from Liam. My assumption is the toll the search had taken on him drove him away, and that he did not want to be reminded of the wasted years searching for answers into his parent's disappearance.

I looked at the board, conscious that this was now a useless reminder of my continued failure. I wanted to tear it to the ground and burn it, but something that deep down inside me stopped me from doing so. It was not that I ever expected to use it again, but the last six years had had so many unexpected twists and turns and disappointments that I had no idea what my future held. I was not convinced that I could let go of my obsession, of my mission, to find Sarah.

What I knew was that I could not continue searching the Redwood forest in the flesh. I exhausted myself physically, mentally, and financially during this search. While I could not go back to a normal life, at the very least I needed to find a way to finance my continued hunt for the truth.

I considered legal action against the military. My treatment was inhumane, regardless of any excuses around national security. I consulted several lawyers, none of whom were interested in my case. I contacted a prominent human rights lawyer and while they were aghast at my treatment, they did not see a legal recourse. We discussed civil action to get compensation. While it might sound crude, it looked like the easiest path to funding my ongoing pursuit of truth. I was convinced I had a strong enough case to at least get some sort of pay out from the military. The human rights lawyer not only disagreed but did not want to handle something so crass. Their mission was to stop the abuse of human rights not to profit from it.

This left me lost, penniless and beaten. I needed something to focus my energy on and to rebuild the mental stamina I would need to start again.

# CHAPTER 27

My internal drive to find Sarah and the truth around the Redwood forest had not diminished, it was only my energy that had been drained. I decided that if there was a cover up by the authorities then perhaps the authorities were where I should focus my efforts. My first attempt was to again try and get newspapers and journalists interested in story. With my added time in detention by the military I thought this now be an even more compelling article. I shopped around contacting various journalists, including the ones that had written the previous hatchet pieces, but to no avail. There was nobody interested.

With the power that the internet and social media brought, I tried to leverage as best I could the foreign concept Facebook, Twitter, and blogging. I have never been particularly tech savvy with computers, but I found creating each of the pages I needed to be relatively easy. Where I struggled was engaging an audience. It was unnatural for me to post regularly or follow up daily on my sites. It may have been a generational thing, but I was not used to picking up my phone every hour and trying to come up with something interesting enough to say to capture a casual scroller. My relationship with social media was stop start at best. For days I would post endlessly trying to get followers, trying to get them to share my story. I would then stop for weeks at a time, almost forgetting that social media existed. This was a lack of discipline which cost me an audience, another failing to add to the ever-growing list.

I was living in a small rented one bedroom flat. My finances were exhausted, and I had to look for some work just to be able to make ends meet. I did not need much to live on or to pay for my lifestyle at this point, however I would not take jobs which were below me. There is an abundance of menial jobs in stores and food businesses. For a man of my intellect and ability this would have been far below me.

I'd spent six years investigating status disappearance, which had created a six-year gap in my work history. Previously I had been a director at a large telecommunications company. With the ever-increasing pace of technology it was now felt that my skills and knowledge may not be at the level required to hold such a position again. I was offered work in a lower manager role, with the opportunity to work my way back up the corporate ladder. At the time I felt this was exceptionally insulting. I would not work for somebody twenty years my junior whose vocabulary was made up of social media trends just because they know how to use an iPhone better than me.

In hindsight I may have let my pride get in the way of my mission. Times became desperate and I regretted not taking the manager job. I inquired with the company to see if there was still such role existing, which they confirmed there was not, but they would keep me in mind for any future positions. As I searched for work, I began to wonder if I had spent the last six years wasting my life. Was Laura right?

I soon came to my senses and realise the ridiculousness of such a statement. I doubled my efforts to find work and eventually found some contracting positions, helping companies identify appropriate areas for downsizing. The pay was good, the hours were flexible and all I had to do was identified disposable resources. This allowed me to not only pay my bills but to start saving for the next phase of my search for Sarah.

Shortly after I restarted work, I decided to approach my local political representative. Perhaps I could get them to lobby on my behalf. Our local politician was a liberal type. She believed in a society that was fair for all regardless of the effort they put in. I thought my experiences and tale would resonate with her, especially if I presented it as a sob story. She was known to have an antagonistic approach towards law enforcement and militarization, an anti-authoritarian streak which could serve me well. While I disagreed with her core beliefs, I knew I could use her to advance my cause. I followed the normal pattern of communication. I called her party headquarters, wrote letters, and sent emails. I saw no response for many of my inquiries. I was becoming frustrated. Here was a woman that would stand up and talk of the virtues of allowing limitless immigration, freeing criminals early and punishing large corporations. How was she willing to ignore the cover up by the authorities in her local area which was stopping the truth from coming out about so many people who disappeared.

Impatience got the better of me. I decided at the next opportunity I was going to confront her. I knew she would have protection wherever she went, and I did not want to seem a threat, so I had to challenge her in an open forum. She was doing a town hall session in the not too distant future. This was my opportunity to stand up and ask the question.

The day of the town hall arrived, and I made sure I got to the location as early as possible. It was going to be busy but doubtful, in this area, that she was going to have a full house. I wanted to be near the front. I needed my question to be loud and clear and I did not want her to misunderstand any of what I was saying. My time came and I stood loud and proud and ask her what she would do about the cover up of the Redwood killer.

"Mr Dempsey, I assume" she acknowledged me "I got your letters, and I got your emails. I also read about you a few years ago and what your beliefs of a supernatural killer were."

It was clear at this point that this was not going to go the way I expected. Her tone was immediately condescending and dismissive. She had the spotlight, and she had the microphone. There was no peaceful way to shout over her and if I tried, I would likely be ejected and spend another night in a cell.

"I think enough of the police budget has been spent investigating your phantom menace" she said. "If you want me to know your story, write a book and I might just read it."

With that I was shut down, and she moved on to the next question. I stood and tried to speak again but was approached by event security and ask to sit down or leave. Feeling my ire rising, I thought it best to leave.

Although I had not succeeded in getting her attention, she had given me an idea. I was going to write a book, and that book was going to be published.

And then the world would know.

# CHAPTER 28

The truth is subjective. Regardless of the facts which you may use to back your point of view there are almost always counter facts which can be used as a rebuttal. There is very little on which everybody in the world would agree. There are conspiracy theories about almost all facts which you believe. Whether that be a religious belief, scientific belief or even a belief about the shape of the world. There is somebody, at least one person, who has a conflicting view. What I am about to write is the truth as I have found it.

I have collated all my experience over the last nine years, and it has brought me to the conclusions I now make. Some of what I am sharing I believe to be fact. Some I accept is conjecture. I have been on a mission to find out the truth about Sarah's disappearance, but I have never gotten to the end of that journey. I may never get to the end of that journey.

All my research, investigation and searching has brought me to this point. What I tell you now is what I honestly believe is the truth of what has happened to Sarah, and so many others.

Is clear to me that Sarah and her friends were murdered on the weekend they went missing. Had they been held anywhere for any time we would have found them, either alive or dead. How they were murdered is a mystery that I will never solve. Based on the evidence we saw in the area, of mutilations and the table coated with blood, it is safe to assume the method was horrific. We may never know how the Redwood killer sanitises his crime scenes so efficiently. It is almost unarguable that this killer has a wealth of local knowledge far beyond anyone I met during my investigation.

During the years of our investigation at least another nine individuals went missing. One survived only to be institutionalised for many years. Only recently released, I never got the chance to speak to Pamela and her current where abouts are unknown. It is understandable that she avoids any questions regarding the Redwood killer. I am hopeful one day she will read this and know that I believe she was telling the truth.

Throughout the time we were investigating residents in the local village actively obstructed our search for Sarah, with the assistance and approval of both the local and regional police forces. They have been doing this for many years.

It is feasible that they are responsible for cleaning up the Redwood killer's mass however I do not believe it to be probable. There is such fear and reticence from the local residents to enter the forest that too regularly visit the exact area of the Redwood killer's latest crime would not make any sense.

The Redwood killer has been active for 40 years. This leaves only two possible explanations. The first explanation is that the farmer's son survived but was so severely traumatised he became near feral and has being carrying out what he sees as his family legacy as he matures into adulthood. The second explanation is more fantastical, and that is for the Redwood killer is the undead immortal farmer. The same farmer who massacred his family forty years ago. It is difficult to logically identify which explanation I believe.

To believe a feral serial killer, who had grown up without any education, would be able to forensically clear multiple murder scenes in a such a dense forest is foolish at best. To be able to carry out such activities is, strangely, more believable with a supernatural twist.

All the evidence, both factual and anecdotal, points to a single killer. This killer is the same killer who has been operating for forty years, unbound by conscience or morality. The only reasonable explanation at this point is that the killer is supernatural in existence, able to move around large areas with stealth and without need for food or shelter. Either would have left significant evidence.

The local villagers and the local authorities know this. The little income the town makes comes through visitors to the Redwood forest. At some point they have decided to trade off outsiders lives for the little cash that is brought in. Their fear of the forest and what lurks within is clear. While not all will believe in the legend, it is beyond doubt that most do. It is more puzzling to understand why the local authorities have written off so many lives without care. One can only speculate as to the true motives for taking such heartless action, or inaction in this case. Without evidence to the contrary I must believe but this is a combination of incompetence and fear. They are unable to prove, in their minds, that there exists a mortal explanation for the missing people. Unwilling to risk their lives for the truth and without evidence supporting a reasonable explanation they would rather bury their heads in the sand. They know that every time someone enters the forest, there is a high probability they will not return.

There is no doubt that my belief in the supernatural will draw mockery from some corners. As with others who have come across compelling evidence of such otherworldly events, I fully expect any authority or blinkered scientist to laugh at the prospect of an immortal serial killer. This is why the Redwood killer has been able to operate for forty years without consequence.

What is certain is it the families of seventy-six innocent people will never see their loved ones again, or get a reasonable explanation from anybody else for their death. My conclusions, my beliefs, may seem impossible to them but I hope so this can give them some element of closure. They would never get the bodies back of their loved ones, but they will know, however difficult it is to know, that their loved ones died at the hands of a monster.

There is evidence the Redwood killer consumes his victims. Between the original crime scene of the farmer and his cannibalistic stew and the table and broken jars we found in our search we can safely conclude that this is why no bodies are found. With the supernatural element of this killer we do not know if he can consume bone as well as flesh, however this would explain the complete lack of bodies. What happens to the equipment of the campers is still a mystery. There may be an area of the forest, a dark corner, filled with camping equipment. There may be even some body parts there. It would be safe to assume if there is such a graveyard anybody who comes across it will face certain death.

The Redwood killer will continue to claim victims as long as people allow him to. Every individual involved in this conspiracy has the blood of the victims on their hands. Their future holds an eternity in hell.

With the pain and suffering inflicted on me, my family, and others like us, I can comfortably say I hope anyone involved in the cover up will burn in that hell. I hope they suffer the eternity of torture and damnation that I have suffered over the last ten years, which I will suffer for the rest of my days on this earth. I hope this anger leaves me eventually, but it is possibly all that sustains me to this day.

When I find the Redwood killer, I will stand toe to toe, face to face with him. Mortal or immortal, supernatural, or human being, he will know fear. I will not back down, and I will not run away.

I will kill the Redwood killer.

# ACKNOWLEDGE-MENT

Thank you to my wife for her support, without which this book would not have been written.

Thank you to my mum for helping edit the book. I hope you enjoyed reading it.

Printed in Great Britain
by Amazon